MALCOLM'S MARTIANS: EXPLO

Terror-Forming Mars: The Journey Back Home

by Jason M. Burns

illustrated by Dustin Evans

Published in the United States of America by Cherry Lake Publishing Group
Ann Arbor, Michigan
www.cherrylakepublishing.com

Reading Adviser: Beth Walker Gambro, MS, Ed., Reading Consultant, Yorkville, IL

Book Designer: Book Buddy Media

Torch Graphic Press is an imprint of Cherry Lake Publishing Group.

Library of Congress Cataloging-in-Publication Data has been filed and is available at catalog.loc.gov

Cherry Lake Publishing Group would like to acknowledge the work of the Partnership for 21st Century
Learning, a Network of Battelle for Kids. Please visit http://www.battelleforkids.org/networks/p21 for
more information.

Printed in the United States of America
Corporate Graphics

TABLE OF CONTENTS

Mission log: August 30, 2055.

I'm really sad. My friend, Daniela, is too. It is our last day on Mars. As excited as we are to go home, it's going to be hard to leave this planet knowing that we may never be back again. We learned so much here, and not just about science, but about ourselves. I feel like I can accomplish a lot after this trip. It's funny how it took traveling to Mars to make me realize that I can do anything as long as I put my mind to it. I'm so glad Dad was able to bring us along.

—Malcolm Thomas

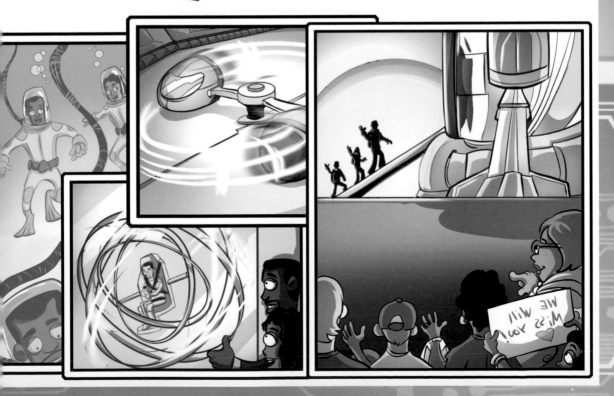

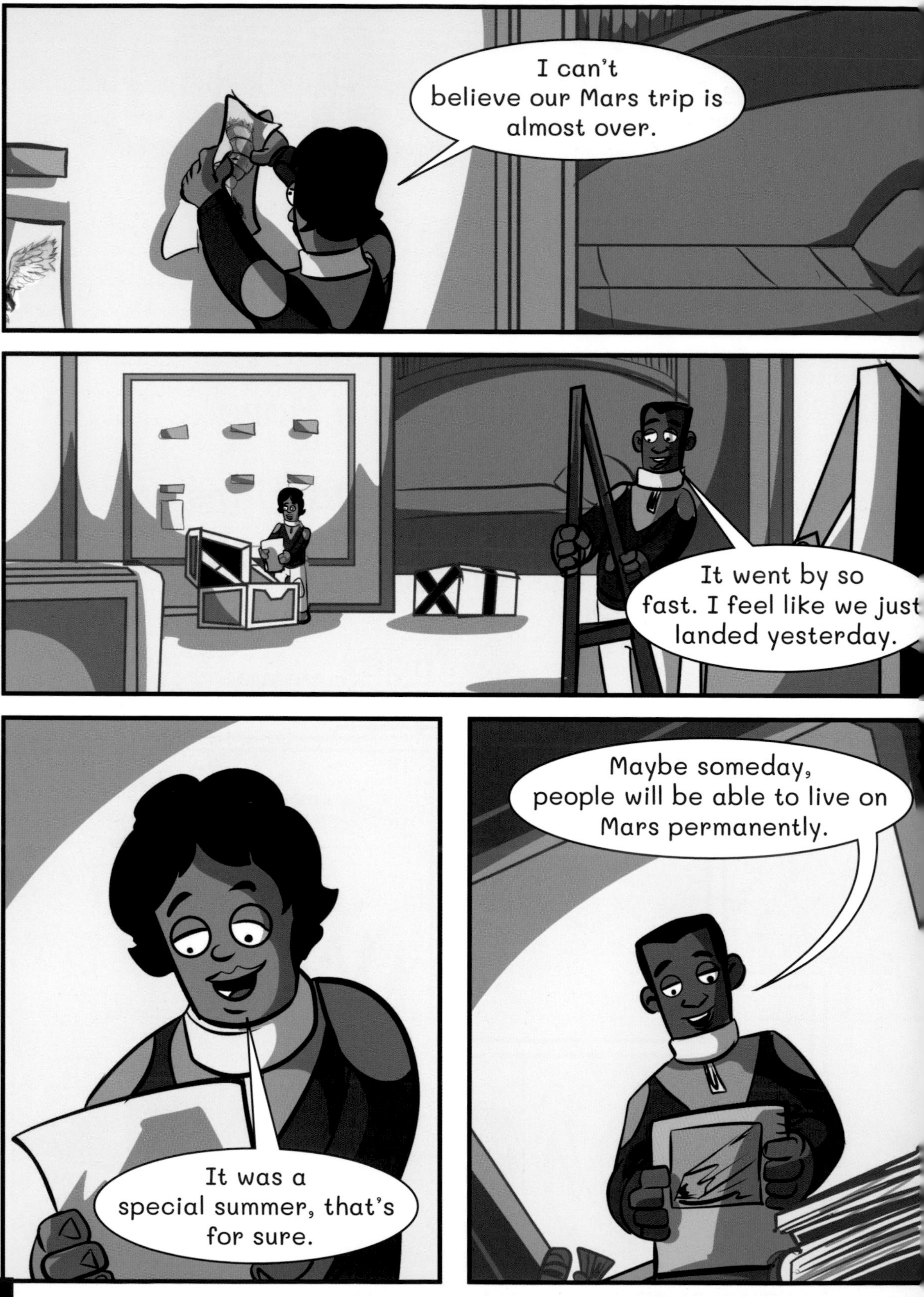
I can't believe our Mars trip is almost over.
It went by so fast. I feel like we just landed yesterday.
It was a special summer, that's for sure.
Maybe someday, people will be able to live on Mars permanently.

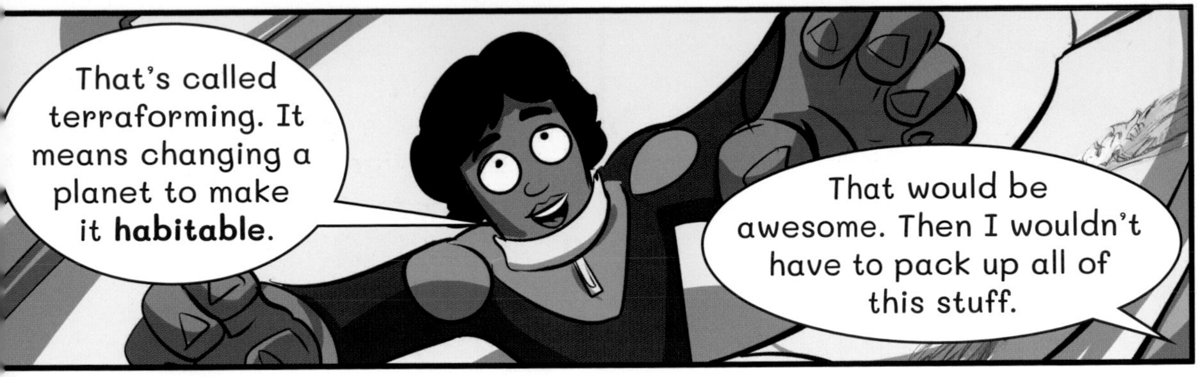
That's called terraforming. It means changing a planet to make it **habitable**.
That would be awesome. Then I wouldn't have to pack up all of this stuff.

MARS FACT

It is not possible to make Mars habitable with our current technology. As of today, the idea of living on Mars is more science fiction than science.

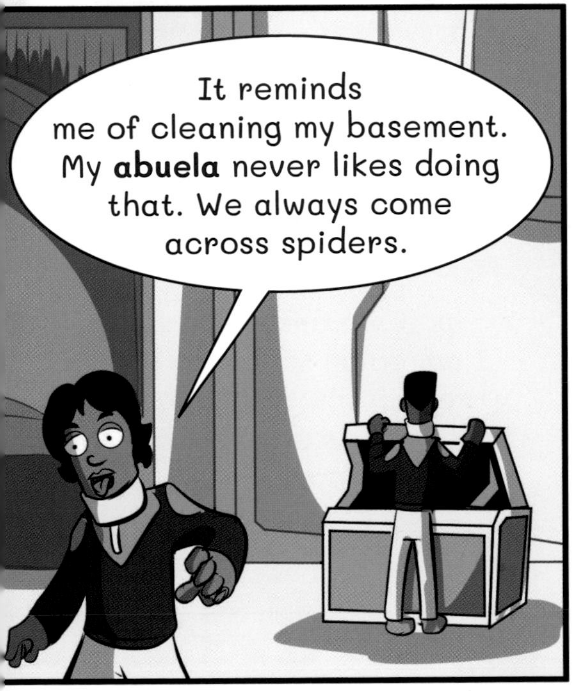
It reminds me of cleaning my basement. My **abuela** never likes doing that. We always come across spiders.

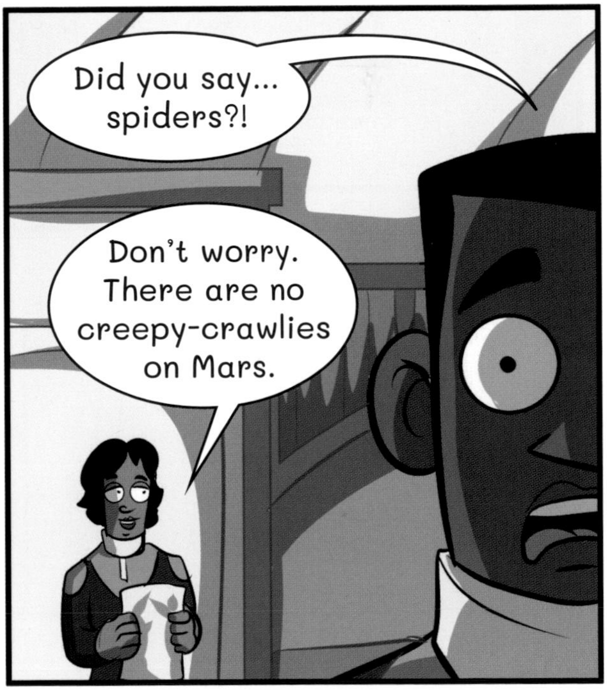
Did you say... spiders?!
Don't worry. There are no creepy-crawlies on Mars.

SCIENCE FACT

We may not have found bugs on Mars yet, but there are plenty on Earth to go around. There are around 900,000 different kinds of insects living on Earth. That's about 10 quintillion bugs on any given day!

habitable: a place that is safe to live
abuela: grandma in Spanish

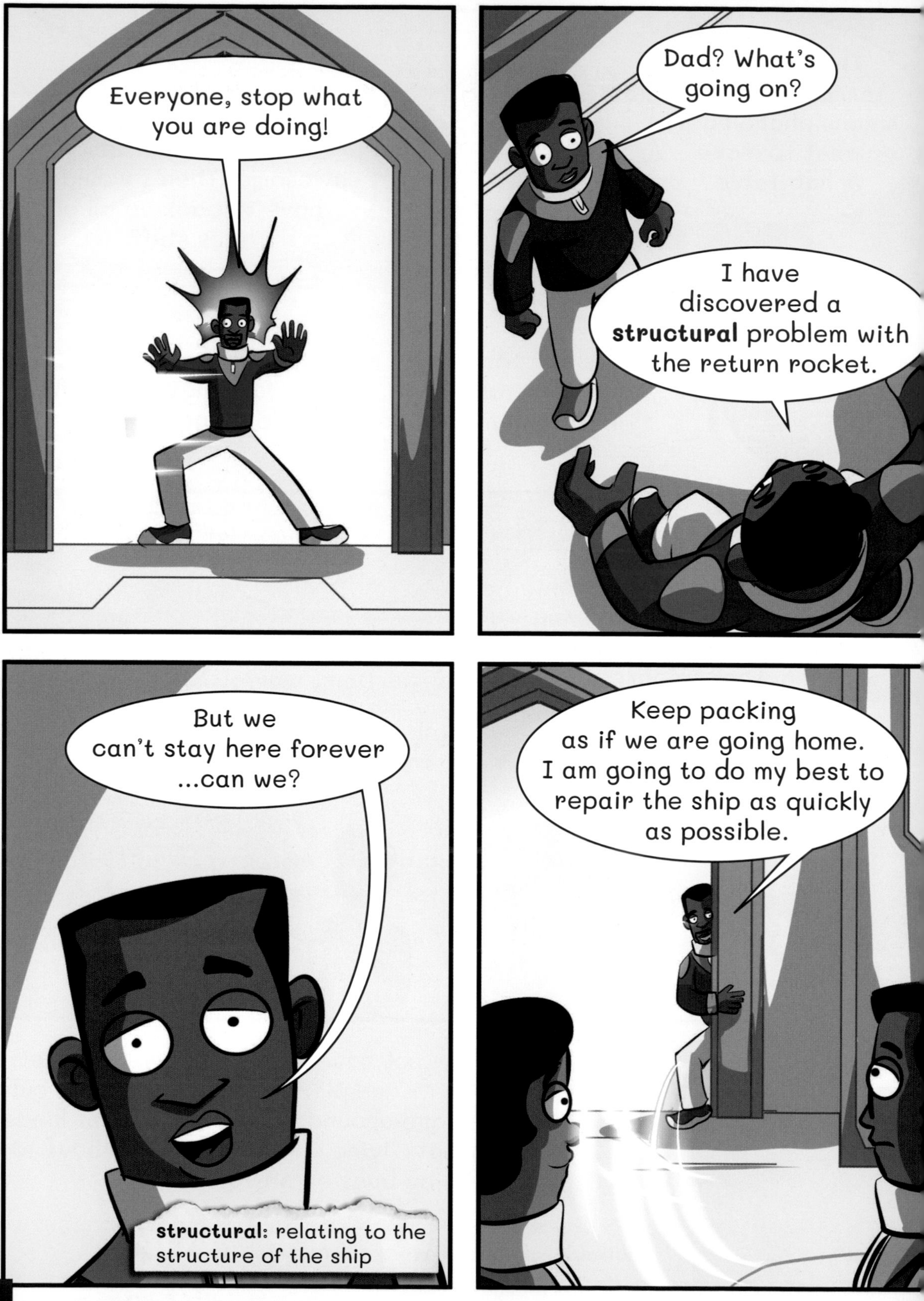
Everyone, stop what you are doing!
Dad? What's going on?
I have discovered a **structural** problem with the return rocket.
But we can't stay here forever ...can we?
Keep packing as if we are going home. I am going to do my best to repair the ship as quickly as possible.
structural: relating to the structure of the ship

THE CASE FOR SPACE

Malcolm and Daniela discuss terraforming Mars. But what is terraforming, and could we do it on Mars?

•The term *terraforming* was coined by science fiction writer Jack Williamson in 1942.

•Terraforming involves altering a planet or moon to make it more like Earth.

•Most known planets are too hot or too cold for humans to live there. Terraforming would involve making changes to that planet's overall temperature.

•Terraforming also involves making changes to a planet's atmosphere.

•Mars's atmosphere is 95 percent carbon dioxide. Humans are unable to breathe this type of air. It is a waste product we make when we exhale.

•Terraforming can also mean altering the **ecology** of a planet. This would include bringing plants and animals from Earth to another planet. Plants take in the carbon dioxide we breathe out and make oxygen in return. On Earth, humans and plants work together to survive.

•There are multiple theories on how to accomplish terraforming Mars. Unfortunately, the technology is not yet available to make it possible.

ecology: the relationship between organisms and the environment

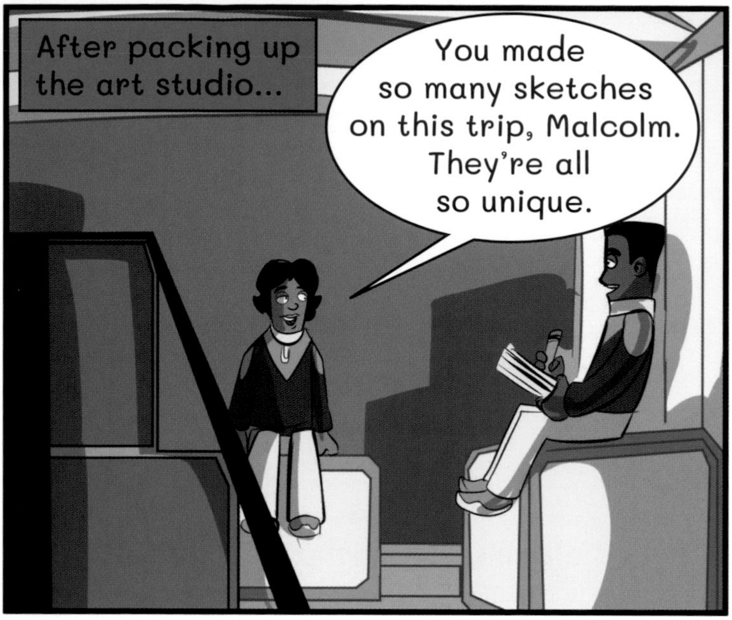
After packing up the art studio...
You made so many sketches on this trip, Malcolm. They're all so unique.

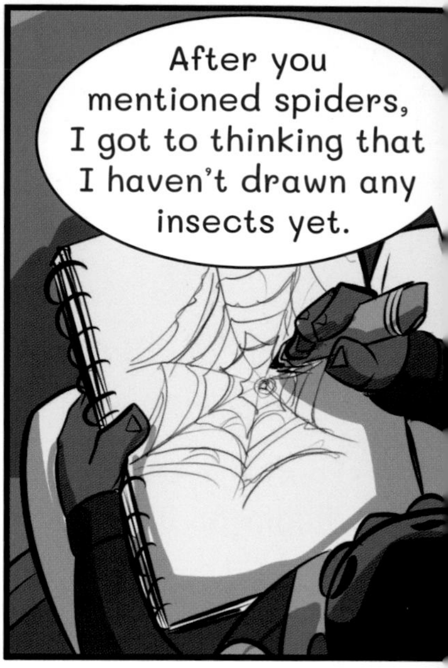
After you mentioned spiders, I got to thinking that I haven't drawn any insects yet.

SCIENCE FACT

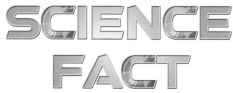

Insects make up 80 percent of all Earth species. There are more than 200 millio insects for every human on the planet!

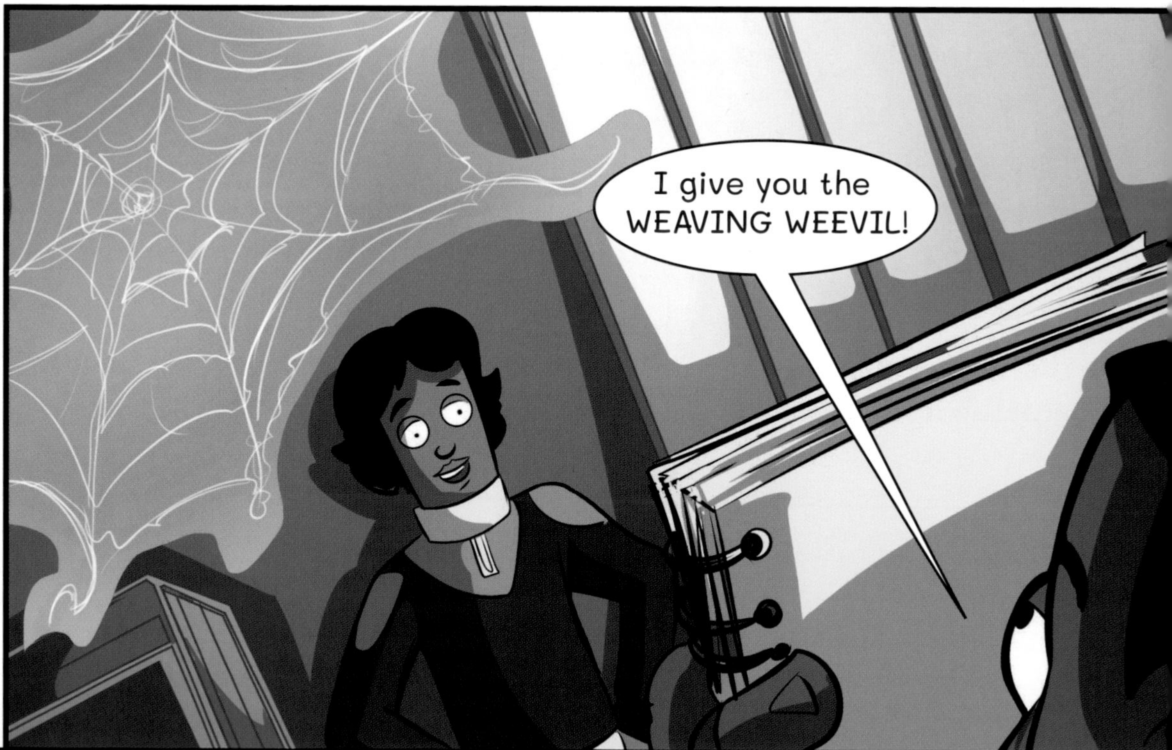
I give you the WEAVING WEEVIL!

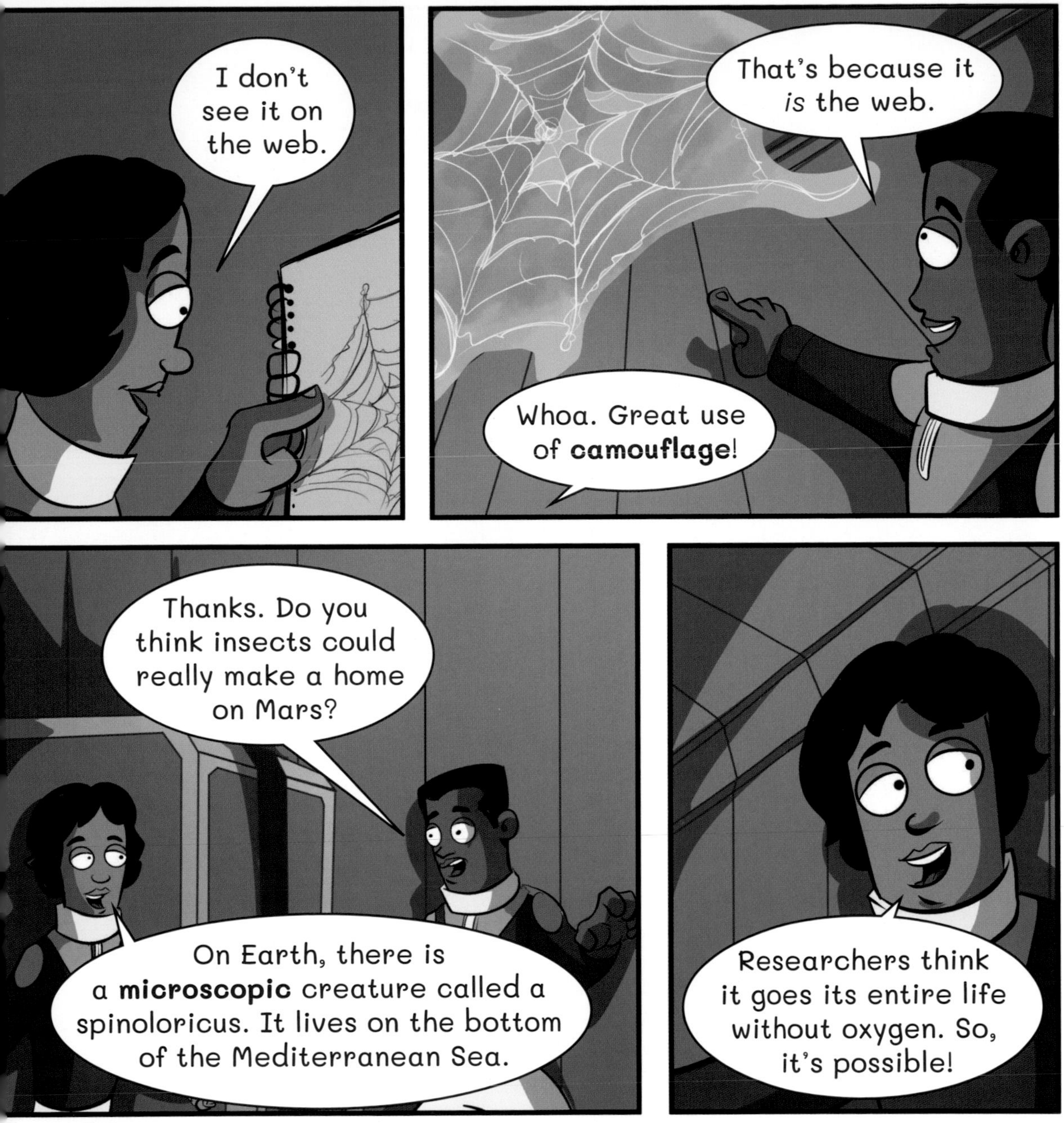
I don't see it on the web.
That's because it *is* the web.
Whoa. Great use of **camouflage**!
Thanks. Do you think insects could really make a home on Mars?
On Earth, there is a **microscopic** creature called a spinoloricus. It lives on the bottom of the Mediterranean Sea.
Researchers think it goes its entire life without oxygen. So, it's possible!

MARS FACT

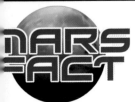

Scientists are looking for ways to modify human cells using the **DNA** of Earth's more extreme animals. They hope that those modifications could make travel to Mars easier on humans. One of those is the water bear, a microscopic creature that has previously survived trips into space.

camouflage: to disguise or hide something

microscopic: can only be seen with a microscope

DNA: molecule that contains the unique genetic code of living things

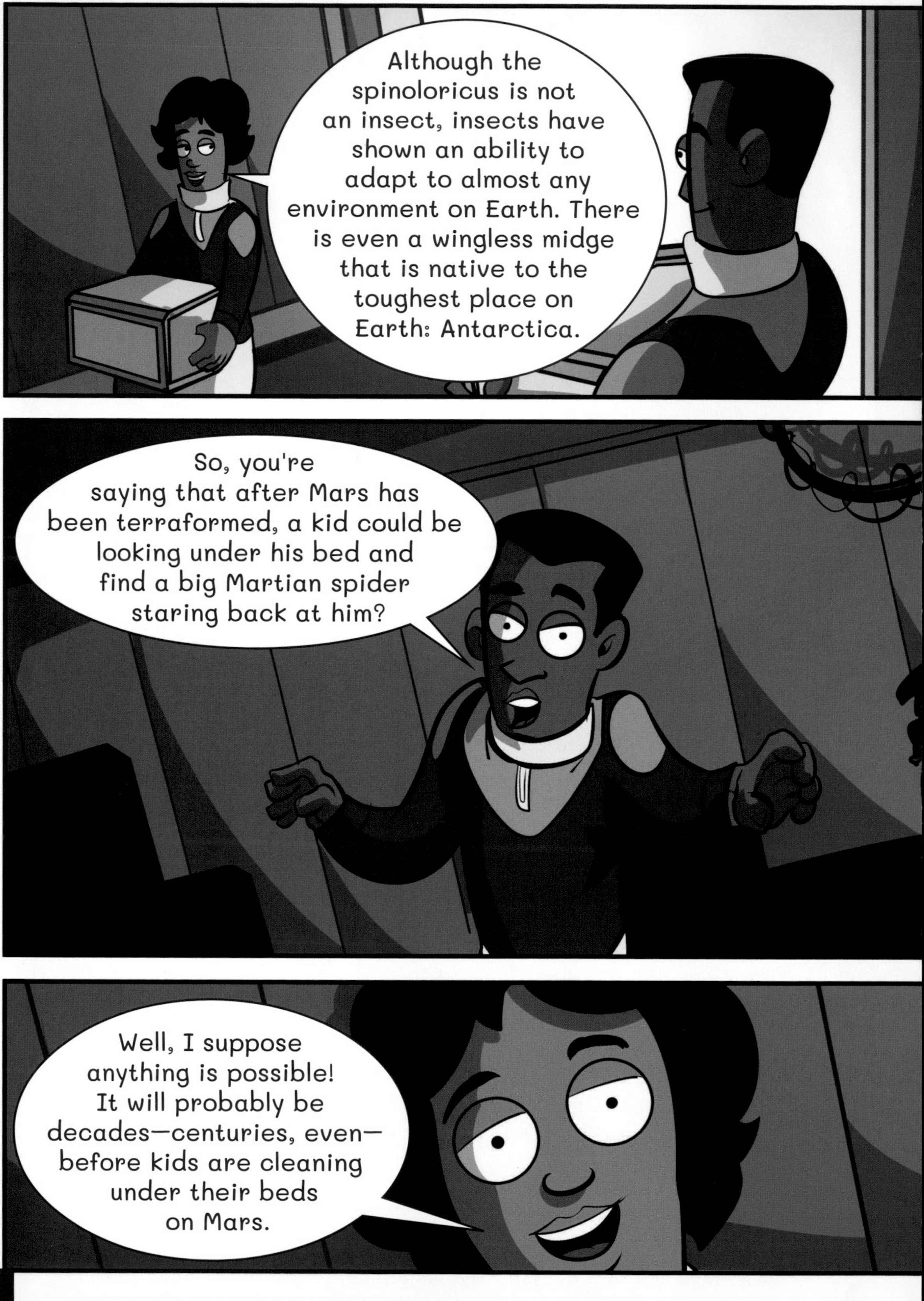
Although the spinoloricus is not an insect, insects have shown an ability to adapt to almost any environment on Earth. There is even a wingless midge that is native to the toughest place on Earth: Antarctica.
So, you're saying that after Mars has been terraformed, a kid could be looking under his bed and find a big Martian spider staring back at him?
Well, I suppose anything is possible! It will probably be decades—centuries, even—before kids are cleaning under their beds on Mars.

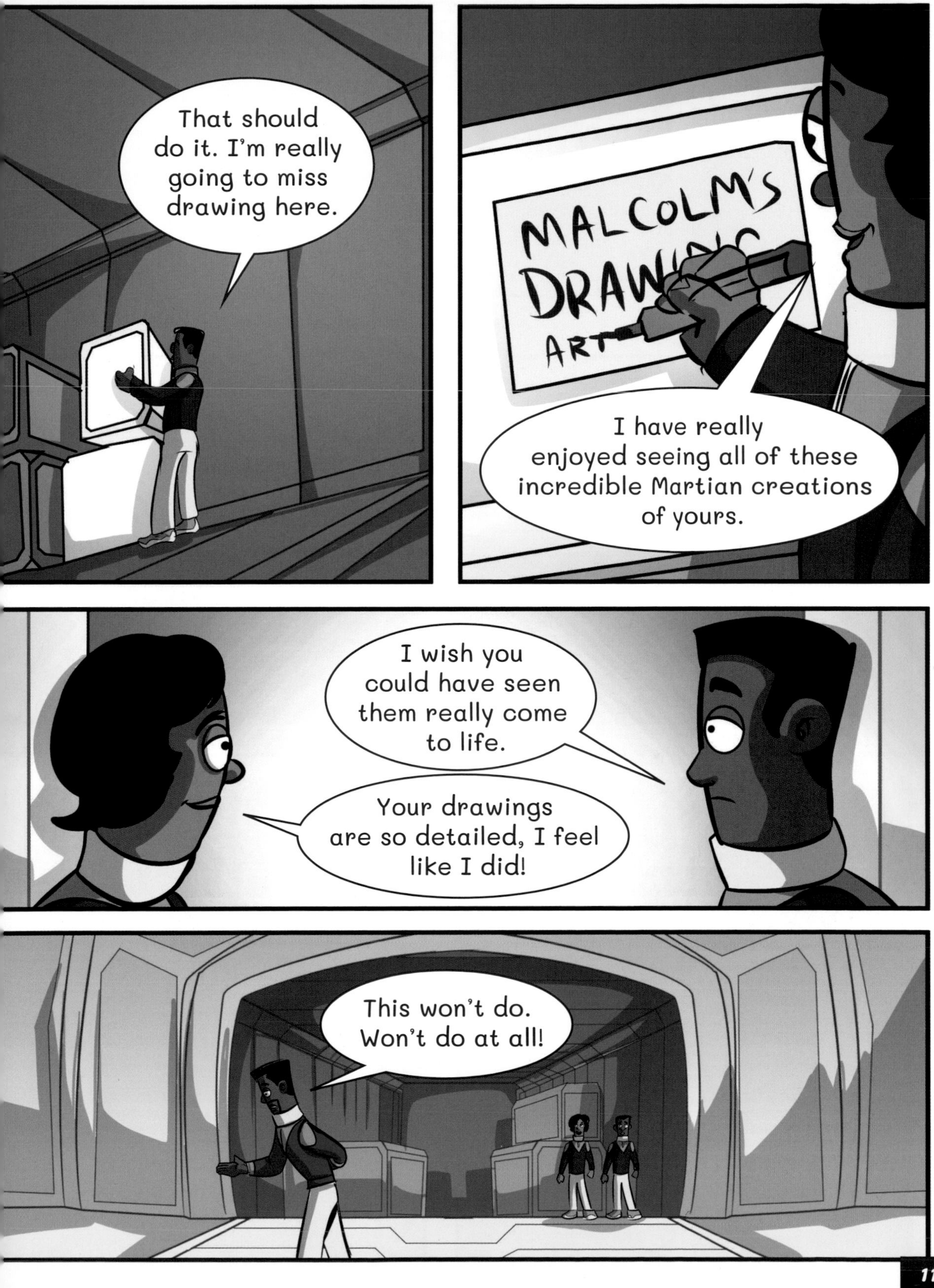
That should do it. I'm really going to miss drawing here.
MALCOLM'S
DRAW
ART
I have really enjoyed seeing all of these incredible Martian creations of yours.
I wish you could have seen them really come to life.
Your drawings are so detailed, I feel like I did!
This won't do. Won't do at all!

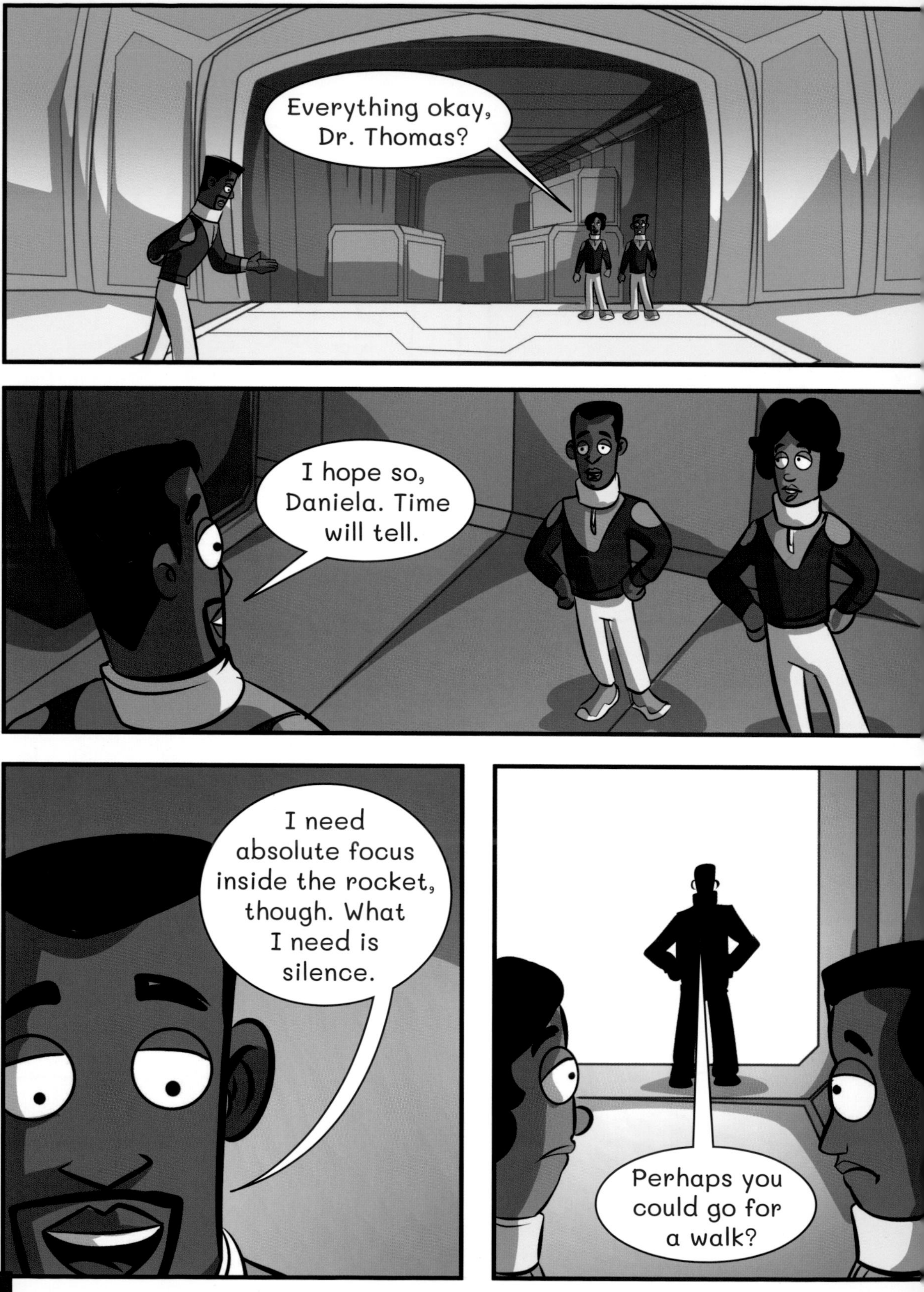
Everything okay, Dr. Thomas?
I hope so, Daniela. Time will tell.
I need absolute focus inside the rocket, though. What I need is silence.
Perhaps you could go for a walk?

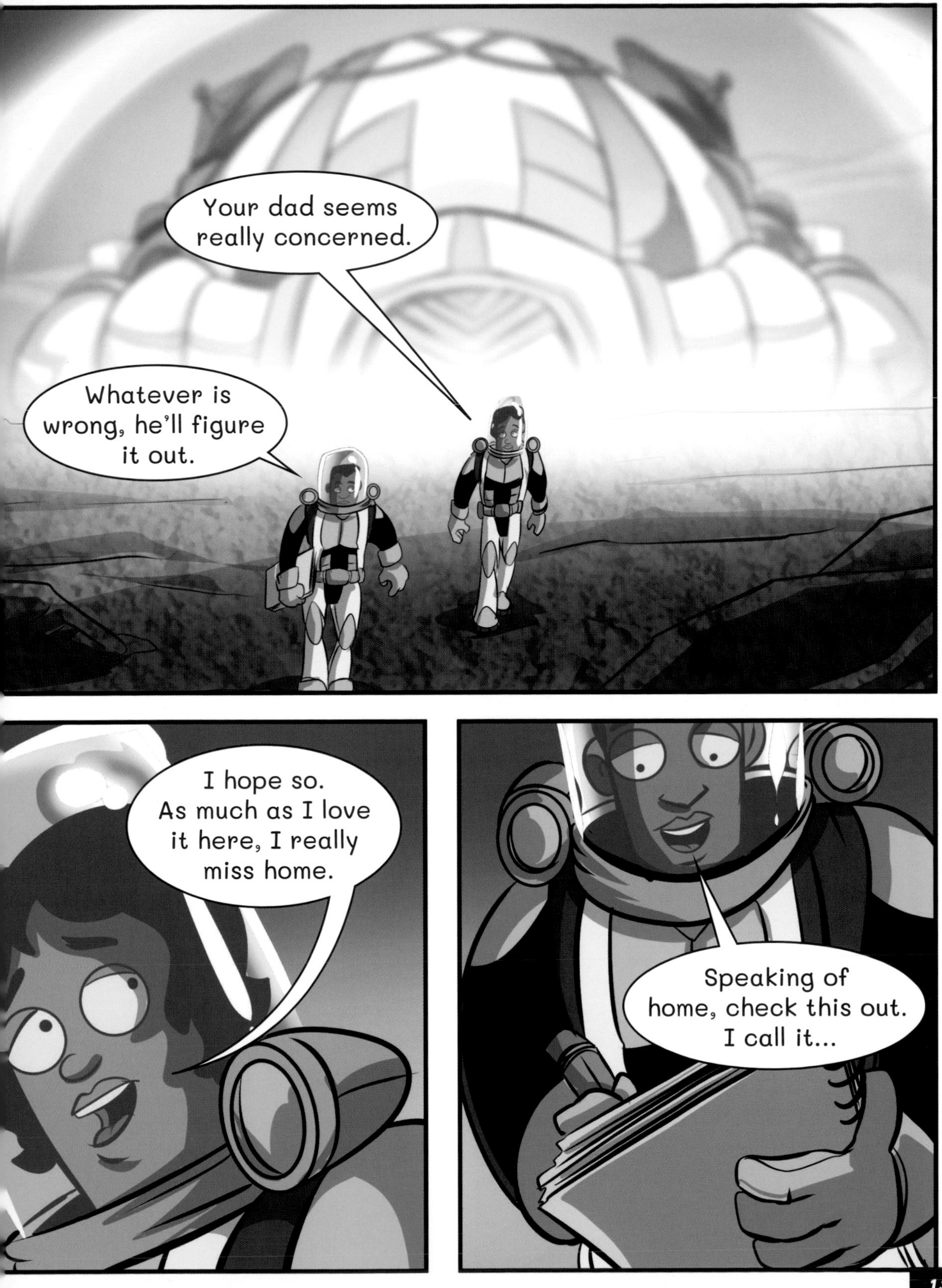
Your dad seems really concerned.
Whatever is wrong, he'll figure it out.
I hope so. As much as I love it here, I really miss home.
Speaking of home, check this out. I call it...

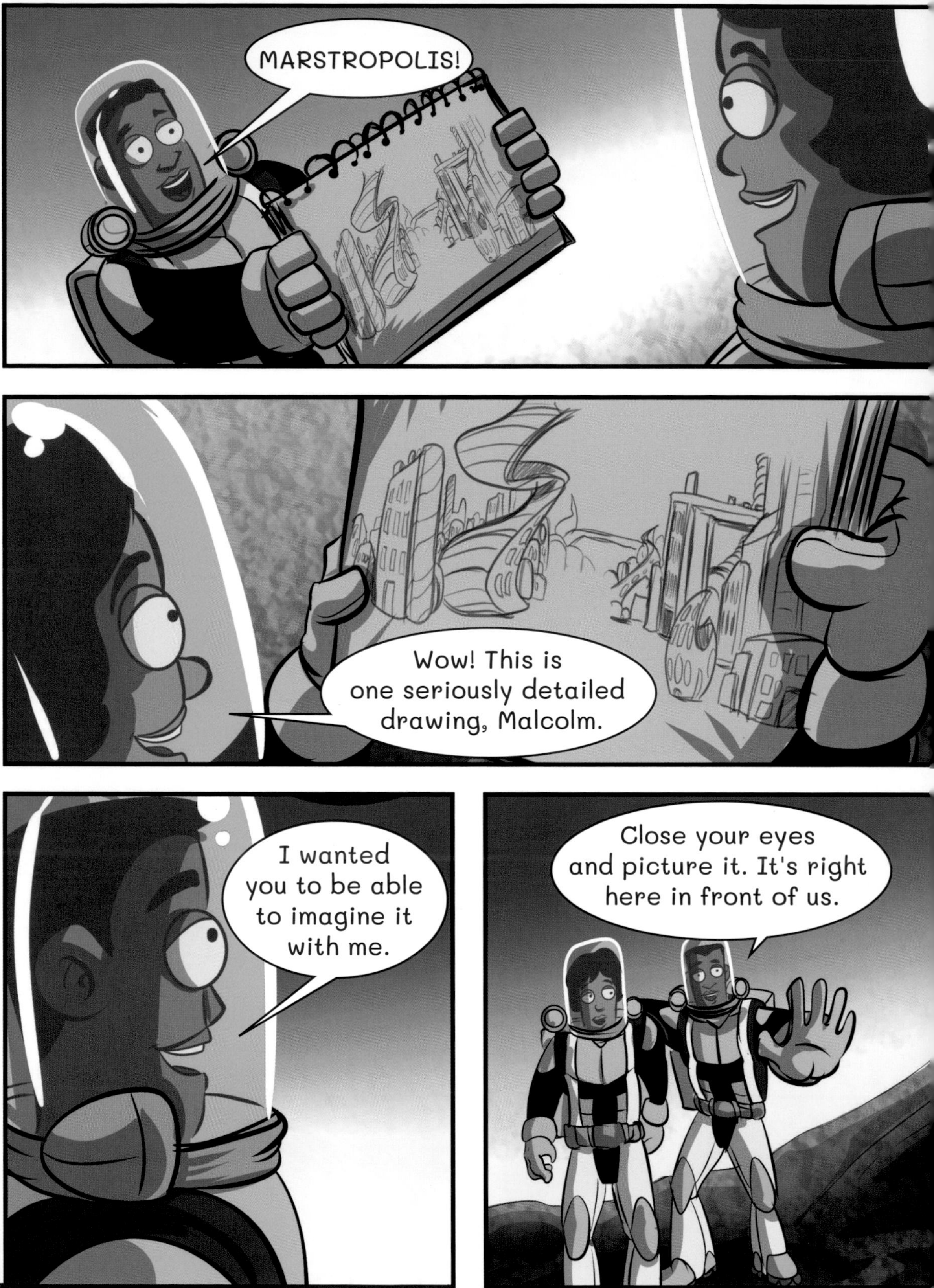
MARSTROPOLIS!
Wow! This is one seriously detailed drawing, Malcolm.
I wanted you to be able to imagine it with me.
Close your eyes and picture it. It's right here in front of us.

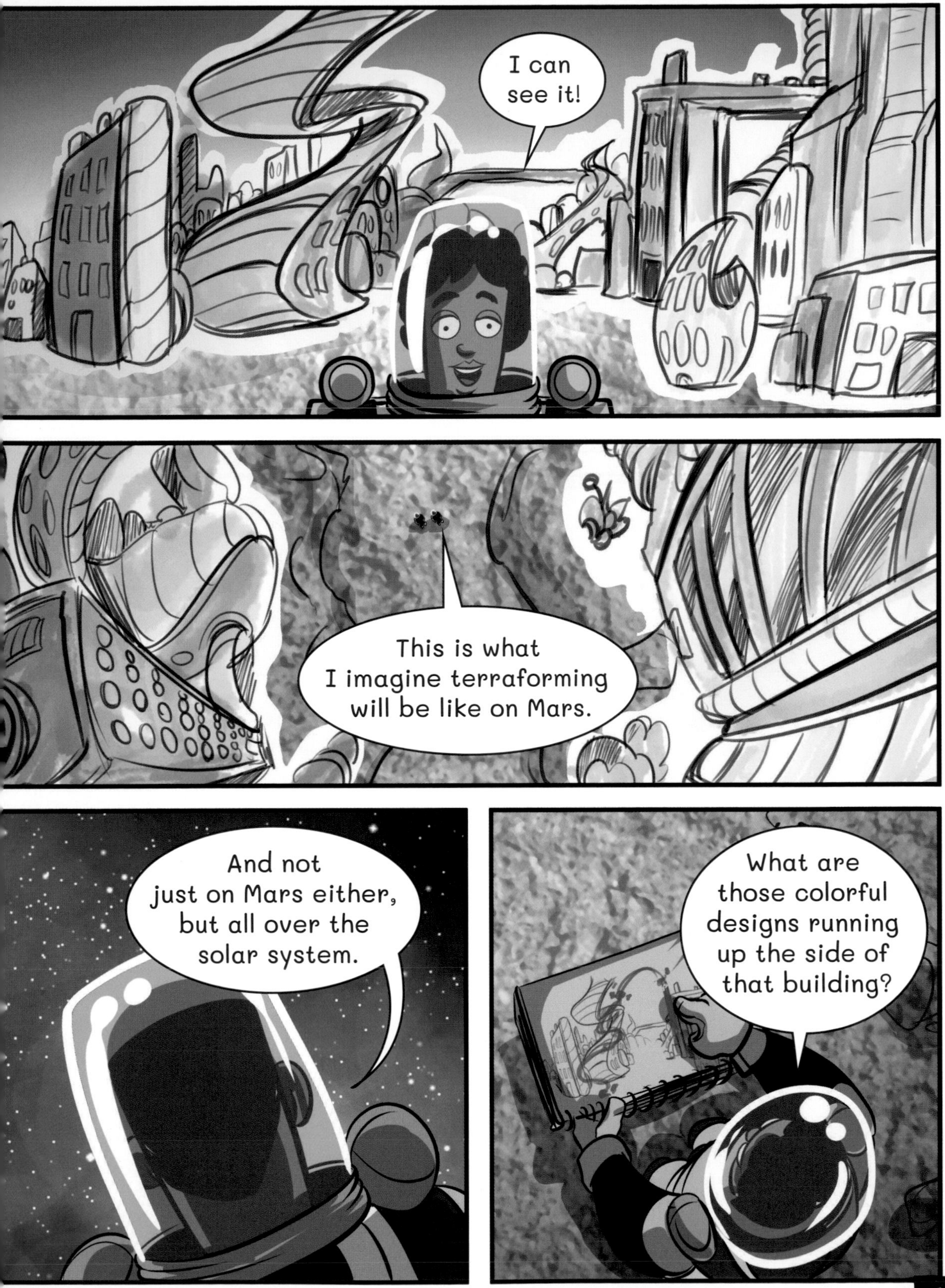
I can see it!
This is what I imagine terraforming will be like on Mars.
And not just on Mars either, but all over the solar system.
What are those colorful designs running up the side of that building?

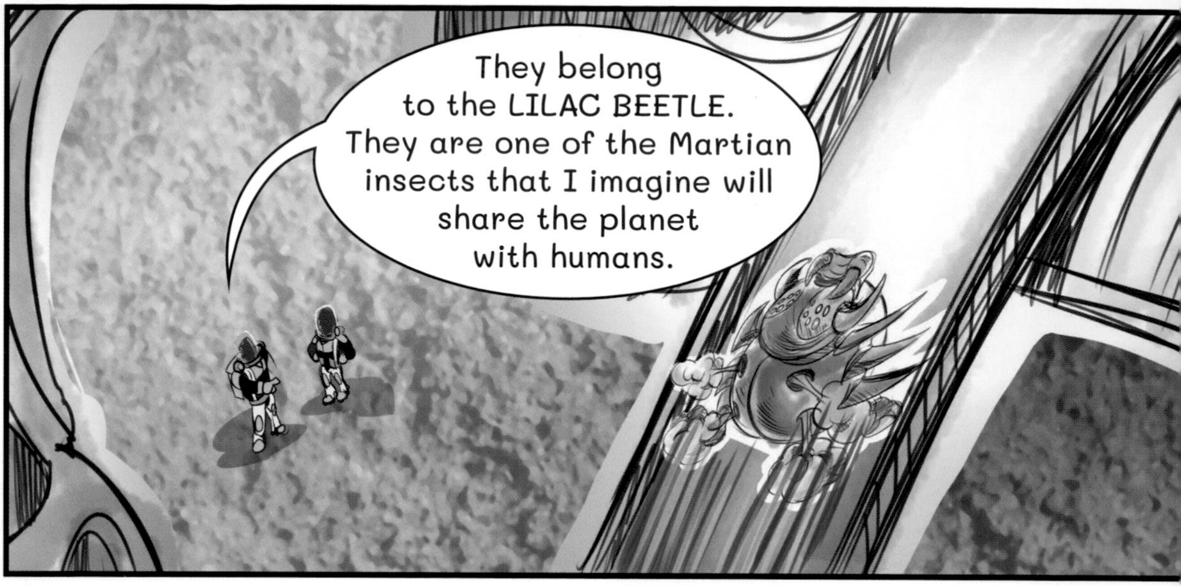
They belong to the LILAC BEETLE. They are one of the Martian insects that I imagine will share the planet with humans.

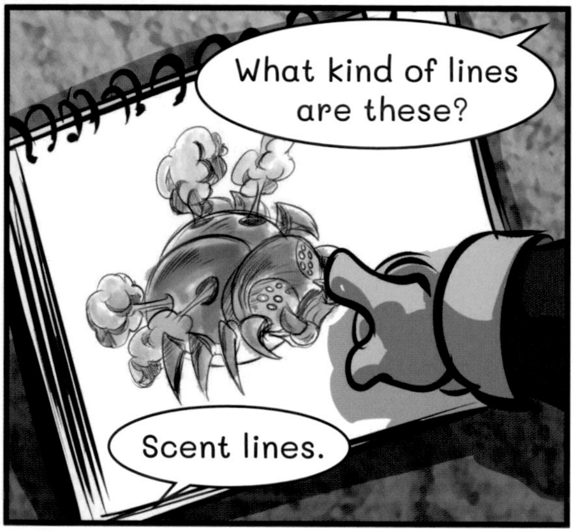
What kind of lines are these?
Scent lines.

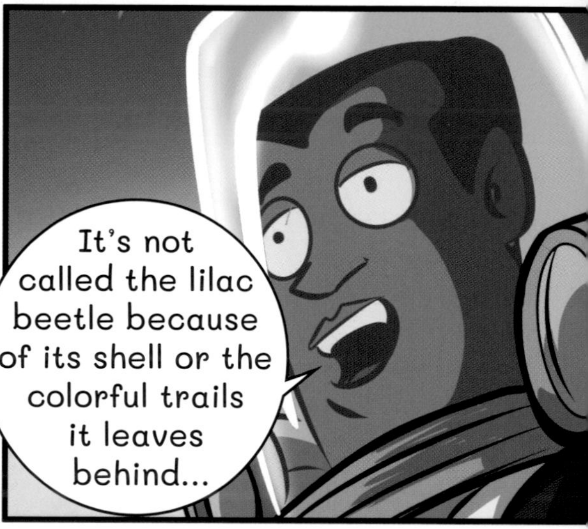
It's not called the lilac beetle because of its shell or the colorful trails it leaves behind...

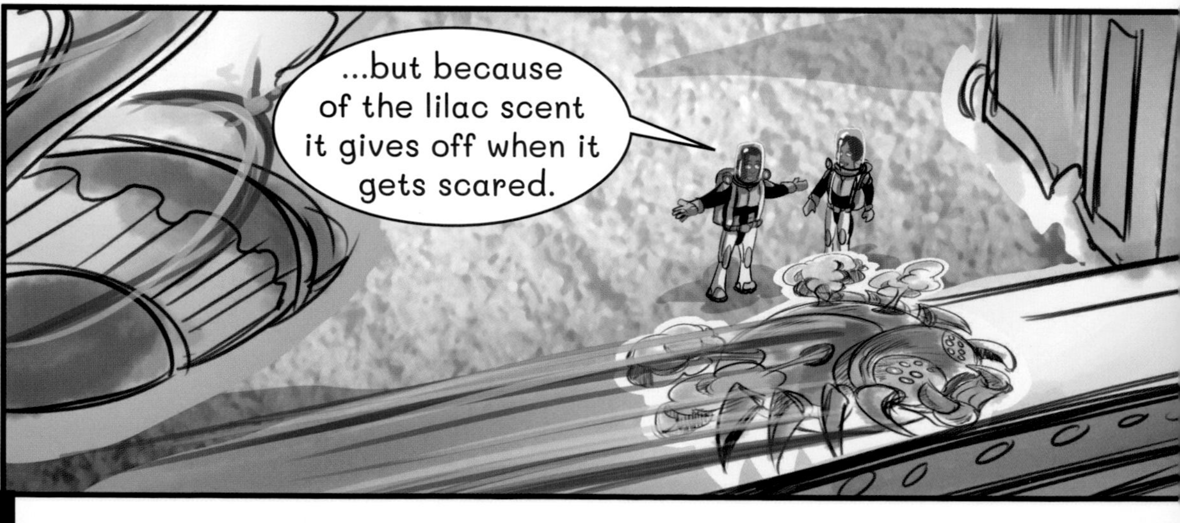
...but because of the lilac scent it gives off when it gets scared.

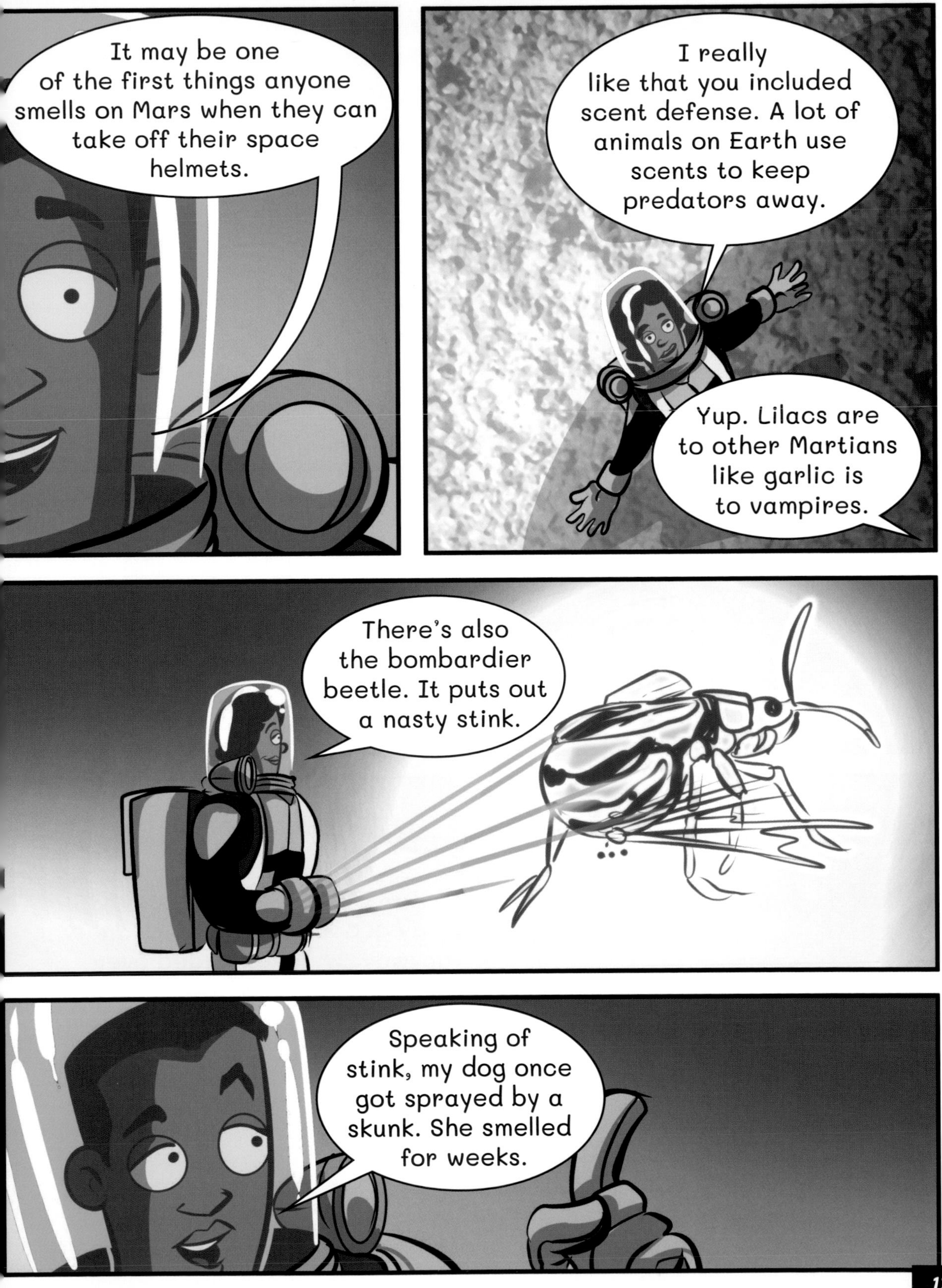
It may be one of the first things anyone smells on Mars when they can take off their space helmets.
I really like that you included scent defense. A lot of animals on Earth use scents to keep predators away.
Yup. Lilacs are to other Martians like garlic is to vampires.
There's also the bombardier beetle. It puts out a nasty stink.
Speaking of stink, my dog once got sprayed by a skunk. She smelled for weeks.

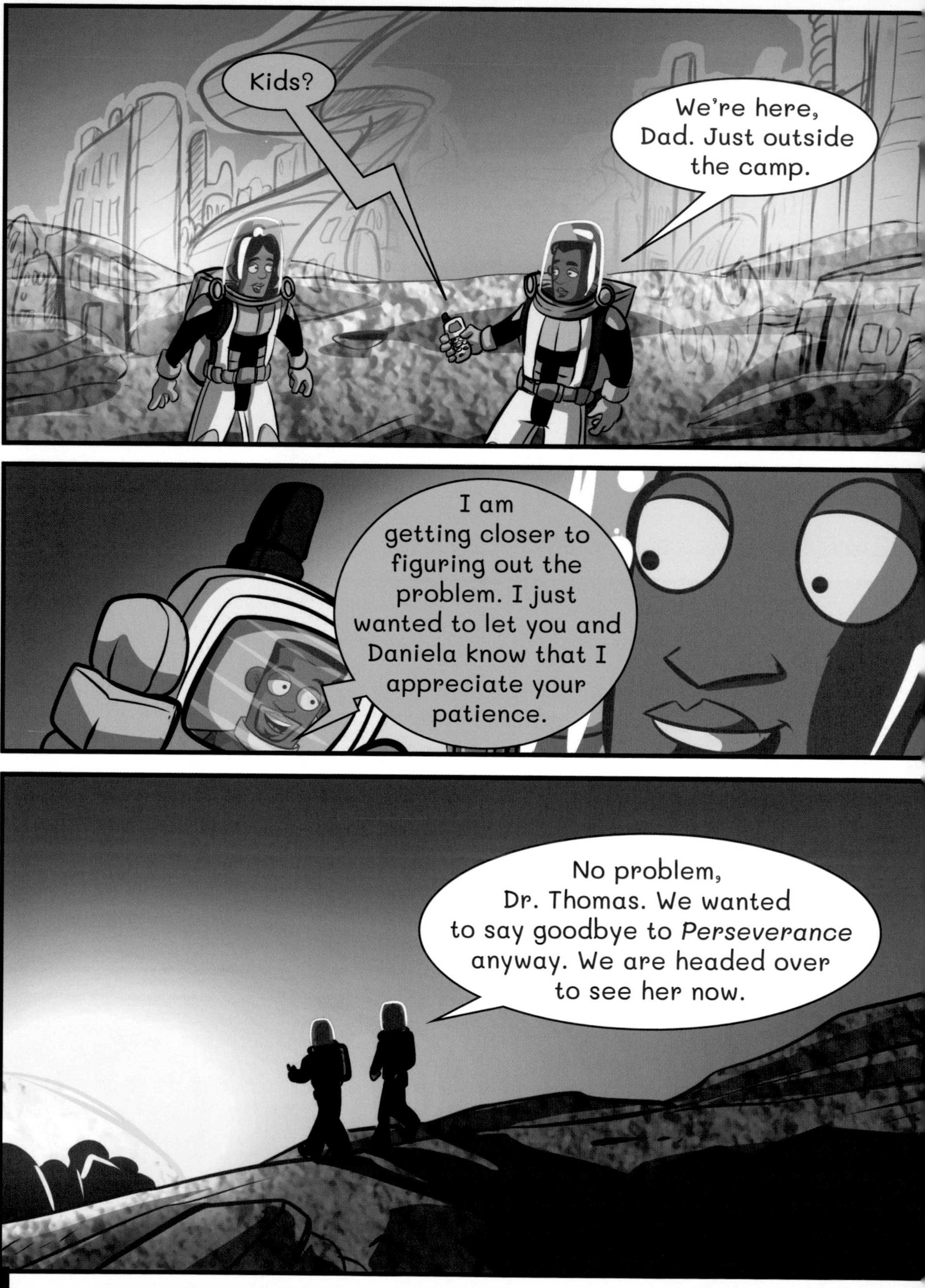
Kids?
We're here, Dad. Just outside the camp.
I am getting closer to figuring out the problem. I just wanted to let you and Daniela know that I appreciate your patience.
No problem, Dr. Thomas. We wanted to say goodbye to *Perseverance* anyway. We are headed over to see her now.

THE SCIENCE OF SCIENCE FICTION

Changing a planet or moon to make it a suitable home sounds like a big undertaking. What does a planet need to support human life?

• Planets within range of a sun capable of supporting human life are said to be in the "Goldilocks Zone." This term was taken from the story "Goldilocks and the Three Bears." These planets are considered "just right."

• In our solar system, there is only 1 planet located within the Goldilocks Zone. Can you guess which planet? That's right, Earth!

• Oxygen is necessary for life. There is not enough oxygen on other planets for us to live.

• Humans also need water to survive. Scientists think that Mars has water trapped deep beneath its surface.

• The atmosphere of Mars would have to be dramatically changed. Right now, it is too thin. It is much thinner than Earth's atmosphere.

• Thick or thin atmospheres are based on the planet's mass, gas **density**, and gas types.

• Mars also is without a magnetosphere. A magnetosphere blocks **radiation**, both solar and **cosmic**, from reaching the surface of the planet.

• There was a time when the idea of sending a rover to Mars was considered science fiction. But now, it has been done numerous times! When it comes to space exploration, anything is possible with the right amount of science and imagination.

density: the measure of mass inside an object or substance
radiation: natural or man-made energy that can be dangerous to humans
cosmic radiation: energy that travels through space at the speed of light

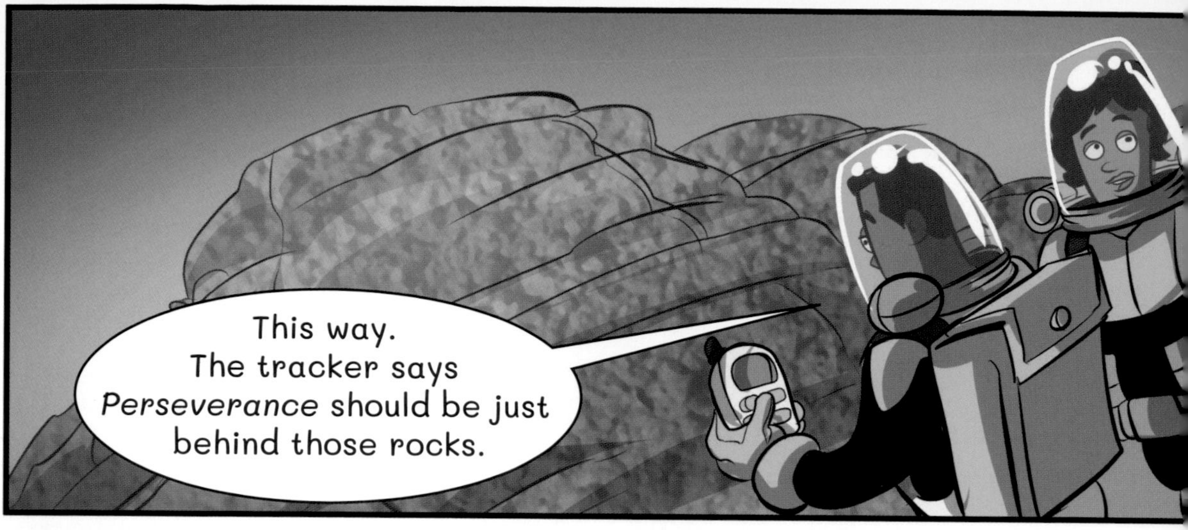
This way. The tracker says *Perseverance* should be just behind those rocks.

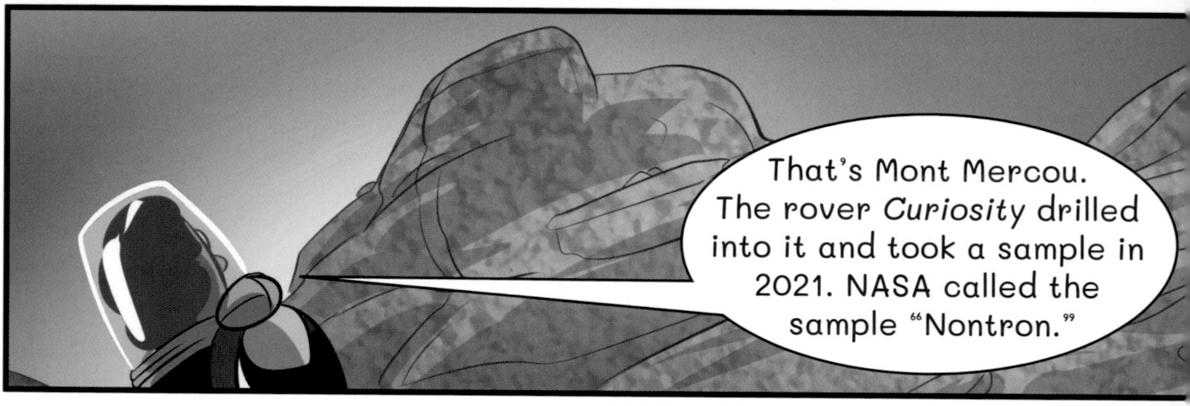
That's Mont Mercou. The rover *Curiosity* drilled into it and took a sample in 2021. NASA called the sample "Nontron."

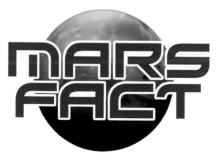

MARS FACT

Nontron is a village in France. The sample *Curiosity* took had a type of clay in it that is found near Nontron. The clay is called nontronite.

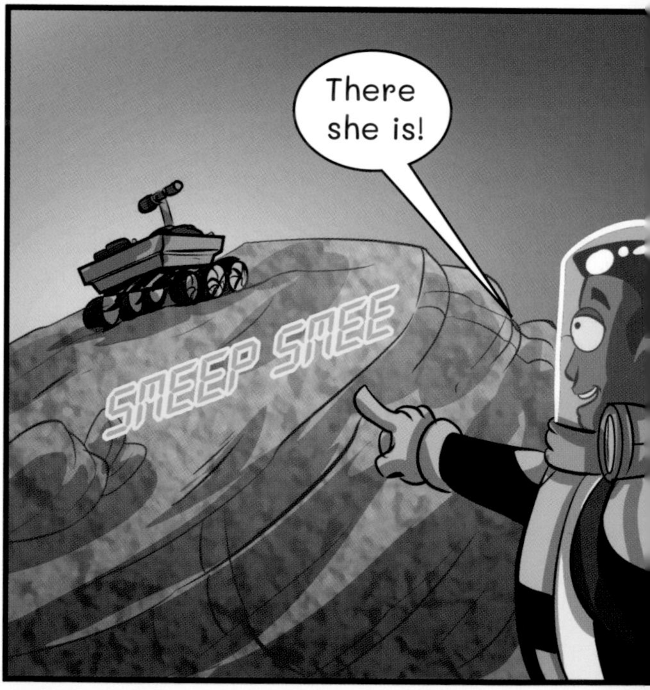
There she is!
SMEEP SMEE

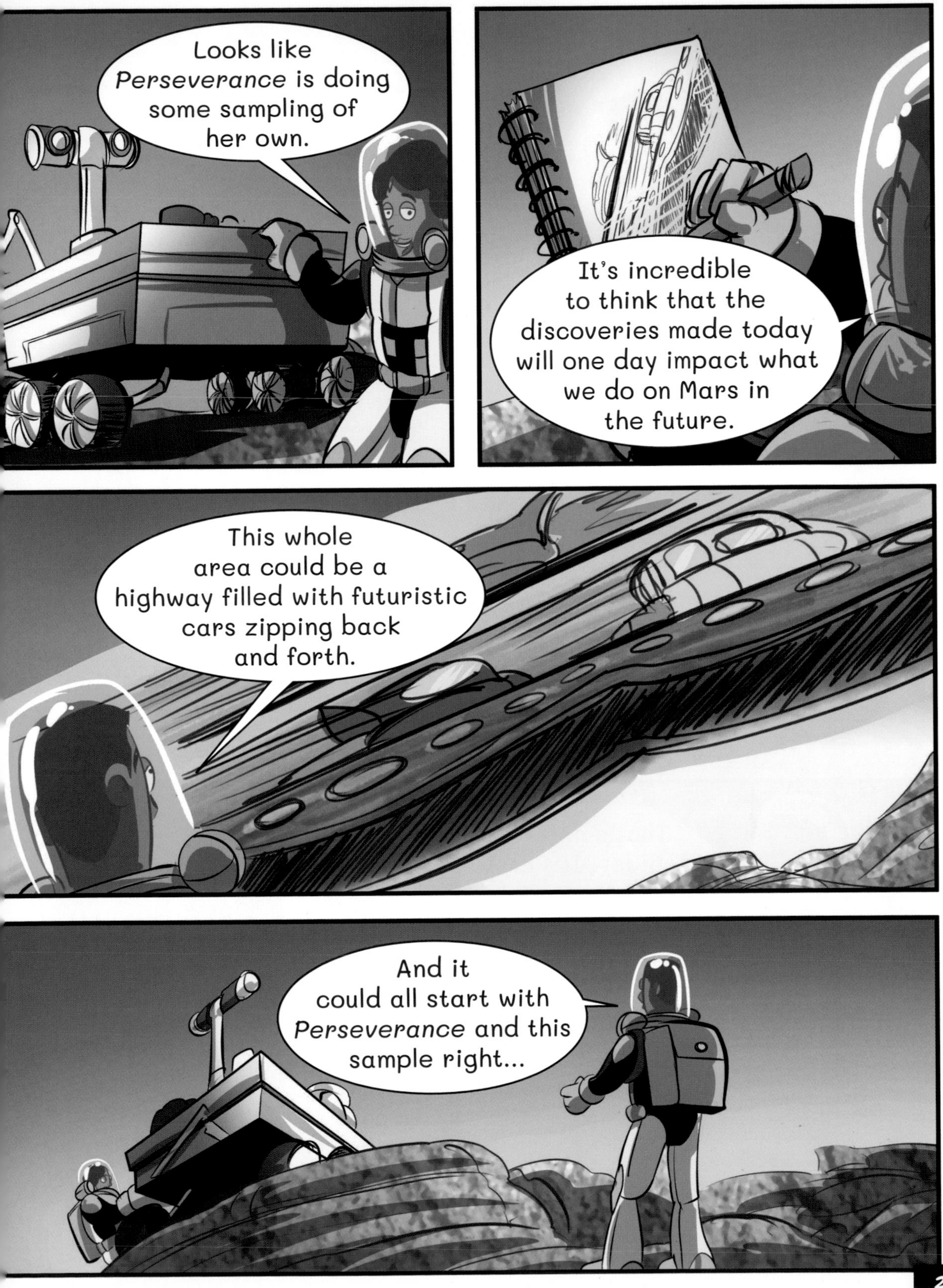
Looks like *Perseverance* is doing some sampling of her own.
It's incredible to think that the discoveries made today will one day impact what we do on Mars in the future.
This whole area could be a highway filled with futuristic cars zipping back and forth.
And it could all start with *Perseverance* and this sample right...

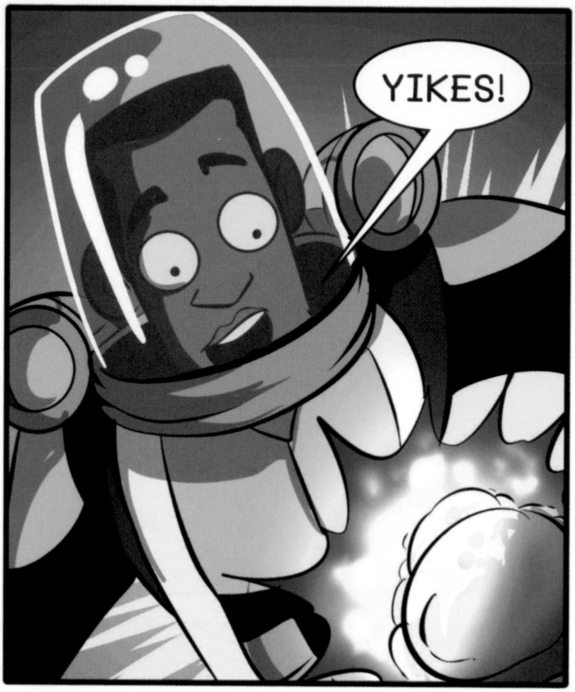
YIKES!

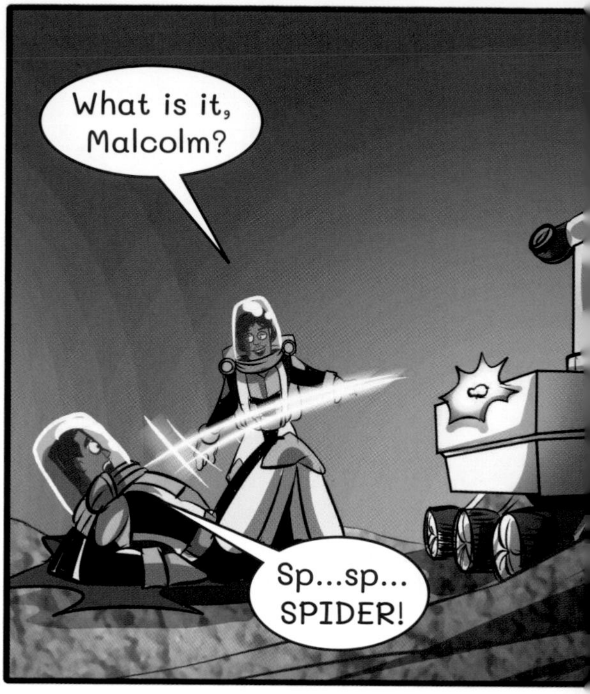
What is it, Malcolm?
Sp...sp... SPIDER!

MARS FACT

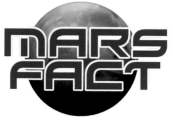

Spiders have been brought into space on multiple occasions. The first spider spacewalk happened bac in 1973. Recently, scientists discovered that gravity plays an important role in how spiders spin their wel Spiders can still successfully make webs in zero grav by using light to figure out which way is up.

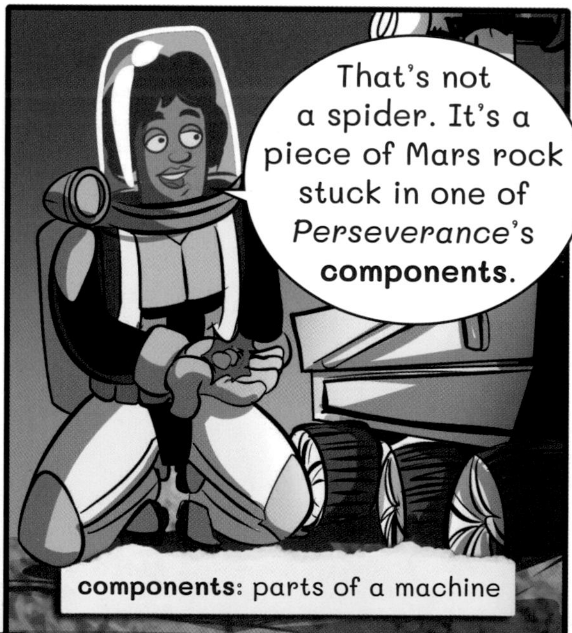
That's not a spider. It's a piece of Mars rock stuck in one of *Perseverance*'s **components**.

components: parts of a machine

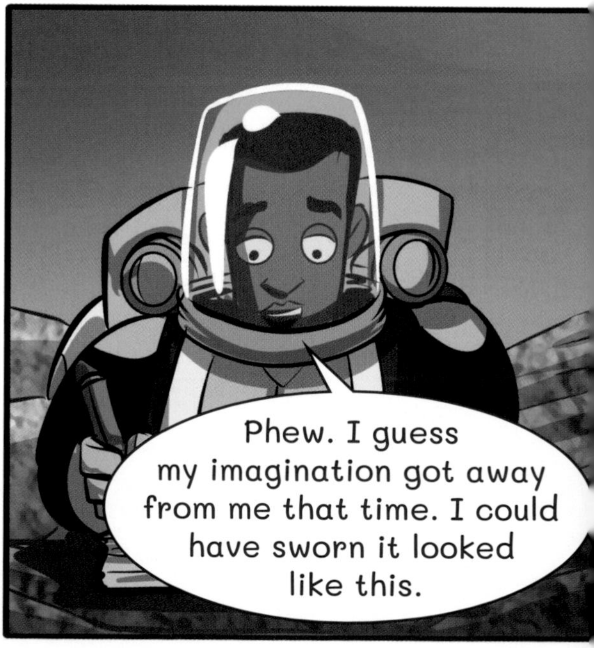
Phew. I guess my imagination got away from me that time. I could have sworn it looked like this.

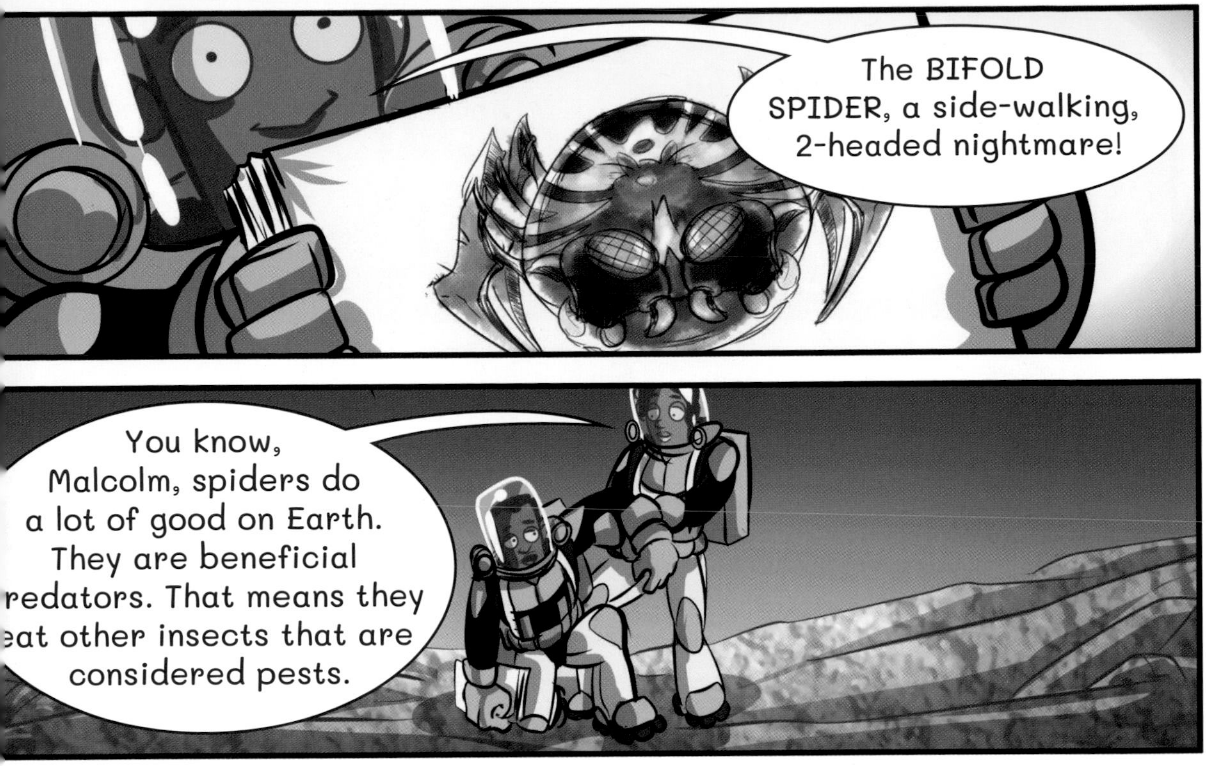
The BIFOLD SPIDER, a side-walking, 2-headed nightmare!
You know, Malcolm, spiders do a lot of good on Earth. They are beneficial redators. That means they eat other insects that are considered pests.

SCIENCE FACT

It is estimated that spiders eat between 400 and 800 million tons of pest insects every year.

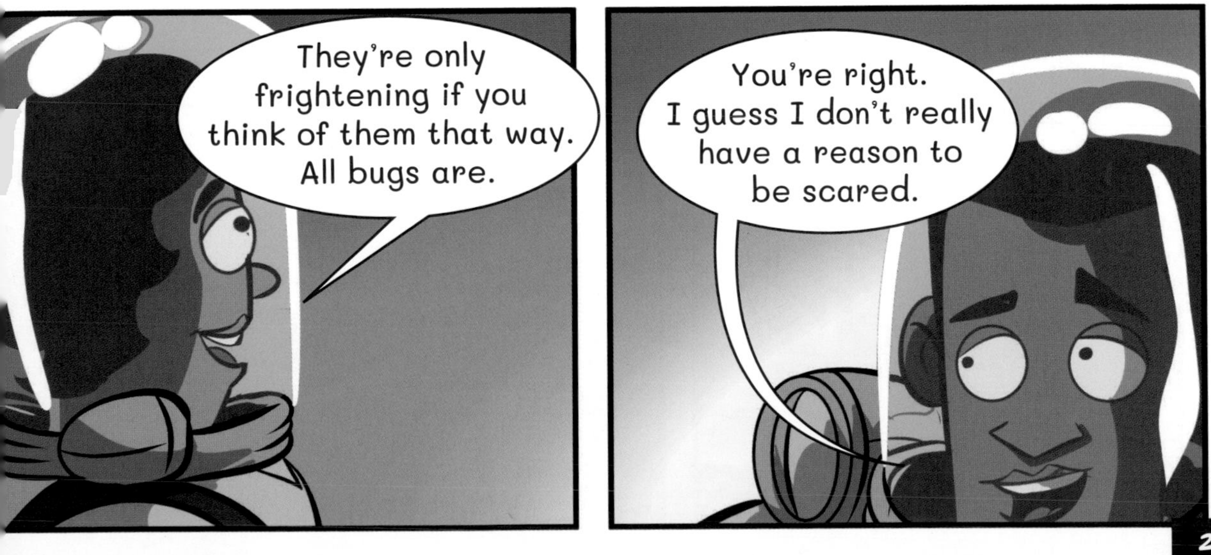
They're only frightening if you think of them that way. All bugs are.
You're right. I guess I don't really have a reason to be scared.

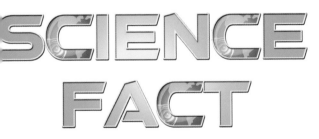

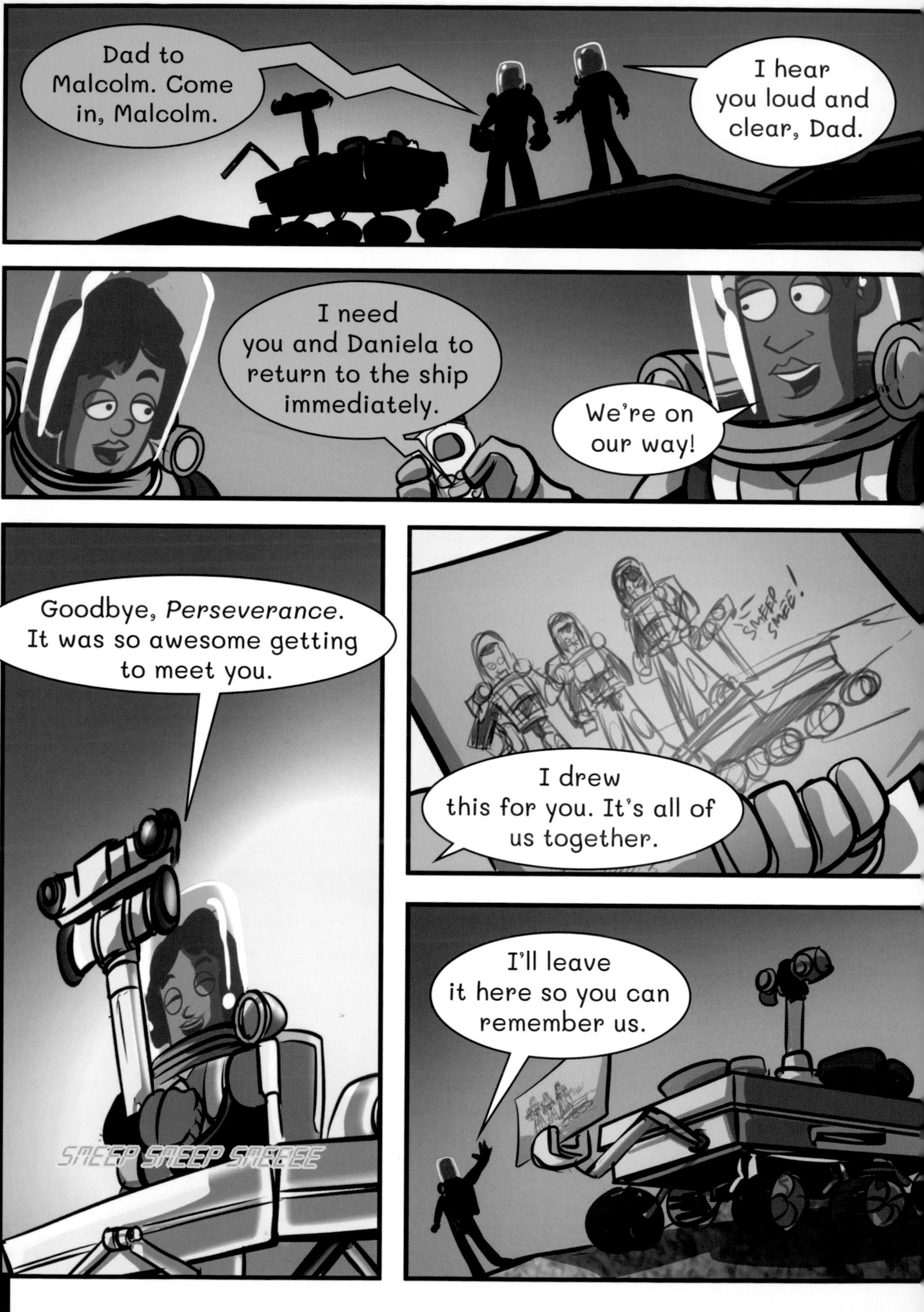
Dad to Malcolm. Come in, Malcolm.
I hear you loud and clear, Dad.
I need you and Daniela to return to the ship immediately.
We're on our way!
Goodbye, *Perseverance*. It was so awesome getting to meet you.
SMEEP SMEEP SMEEEE
I drew this for you. It's all of us together.
I'll leave it here so you can remember us.

THE FUNDAMENTALS OF ART

Let's put the FUN in the fundamentals of art by learning how to tap into the most important tool in your artist toolbox—your imagination! It takes more than technical know-how to draw and paint. Creativity isn't something that can be ordered online. It is something that is inside all of us. There are ways discover yours. Here are some tips to unlocking your full creative potential!

•Limit the distractions around you. In order to let your mind drift away to the ultimate creative place, you need to let it focus. Shut off the television, avoid the video games, and stop refreshing that social media page.

•Surround yourself with other creative people. The incredible work that others do will inspire you to do your own incredible things.

•Brainstorm. Put every idea you have down on a piece of paper. Some of it may work and some of it may not. The beauty of brainstorming is that even the unused ideas can lead to new creative avenues.

•Take risks. If you want to draw a lion in a clown suit driving a bus, try it! You won't know if it works until you give your idea life.

•Discover your inspiration. It might be music. It might be the outdoors. Find the thing that opens the door to your imagination. It's not the same for everybody. When you come across it, you'll know.

ARTIST TIP: If you are feeling stuck or have an "artist's block," try taking a creative break. Read a book, play a video game, or watch a movie. Art often inspires art. Relax and give your imagination a rest.

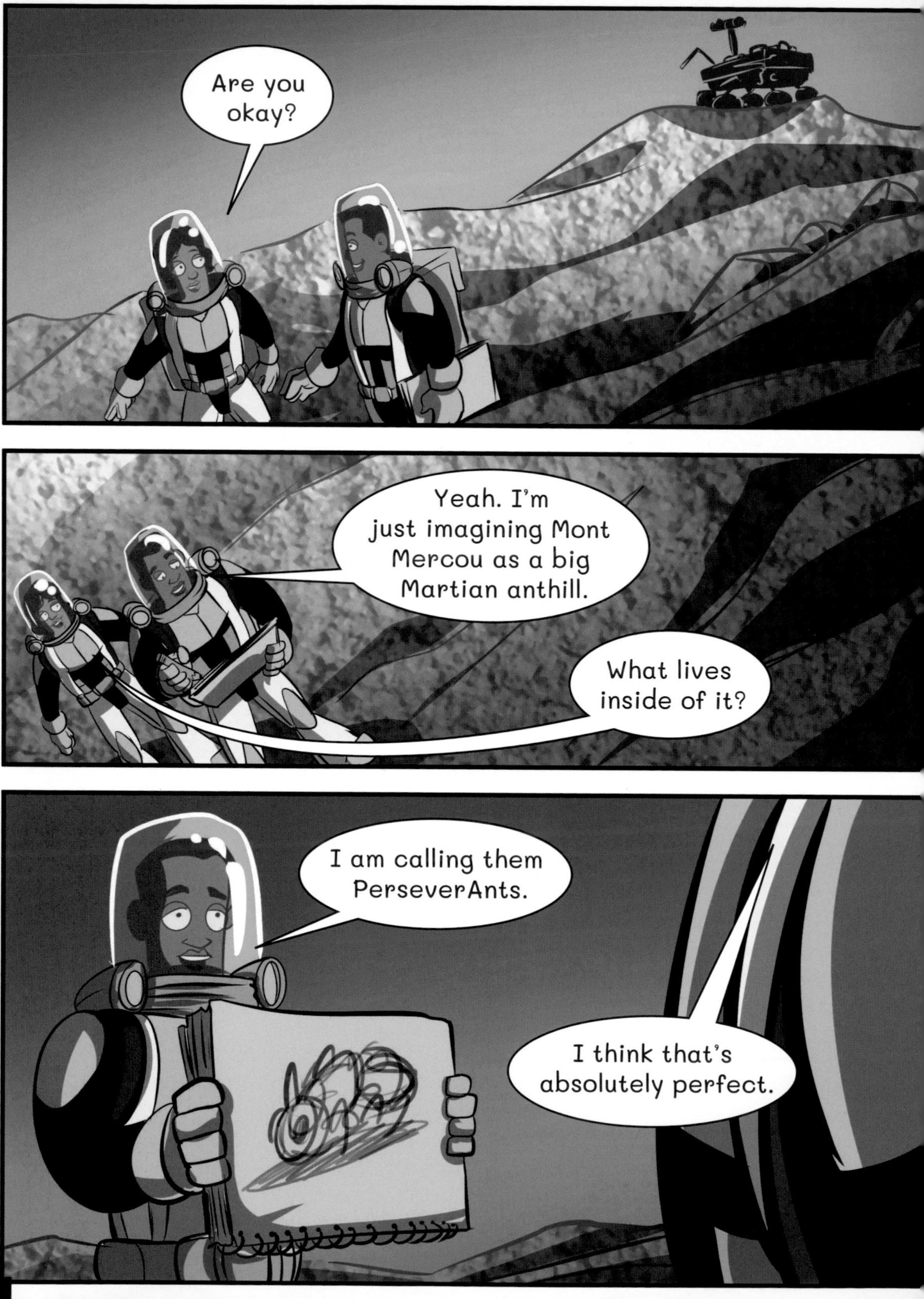
Are you okay?
Yeah. I'm just imagining Mont Mercou as a big Martian anthill.
What lives inside of it?
I am calling them PerseverAnts.
I think that's absolutely perfect.

MARS SURVIVAL TIPS

You're trapped with no way home. A rescue team is on its way, but you're a long way from being pulled to safety. How do you survive? Whether you're on Mars or lost in the woods, there are things you can do to make a long-term stay a little easier.

•Dress right! You don't want to be too hot or too cold. Try to avoid wasting your body's energy on shivering or sweating. Protect yourself from sun, rain, and, if on Mars, radiation.

•Eventually, food and water will run out. Start conserving immediately. Record how much you go through every day.

•Even with **rationing**, you'll need more supplies. You can live longer without food than you can without water. Start looking for a water source immediately.

•If it looks like you might be there a while, try preserving food for later. Dried food lasts a lot longer than fresh.

•Don't count on technology to lead the rescue team to you. Use rocks to spell "SOS" on the ground as large as you can. This will help rescuers see you from overhead.

•SOS doesn't actually stand for anything. It was originally a distress signal sent in **Morse code**. It was later adopted as an international symbol for "Help!"

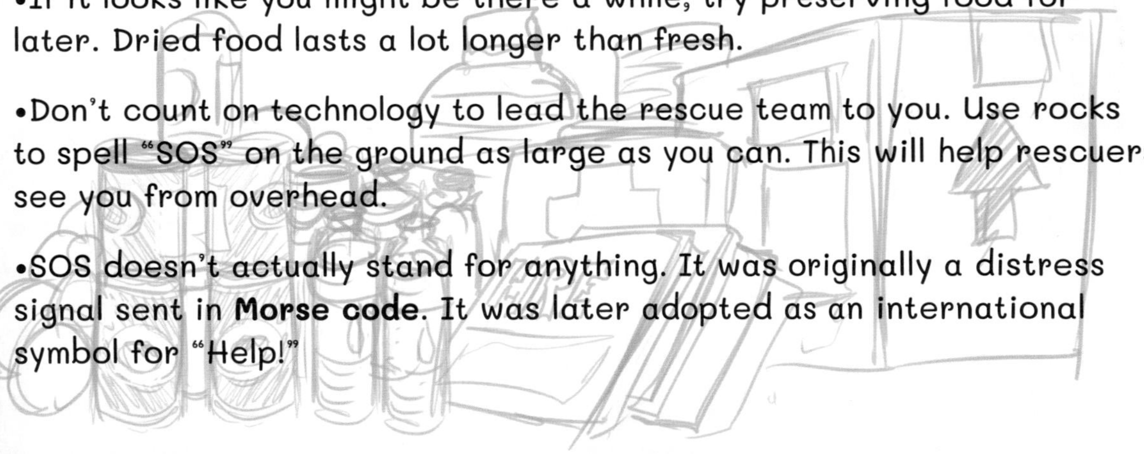

rationing: eating or drinking a set amount

Morse code: a system of communication that uses dots and dashes to represent letters and numbers

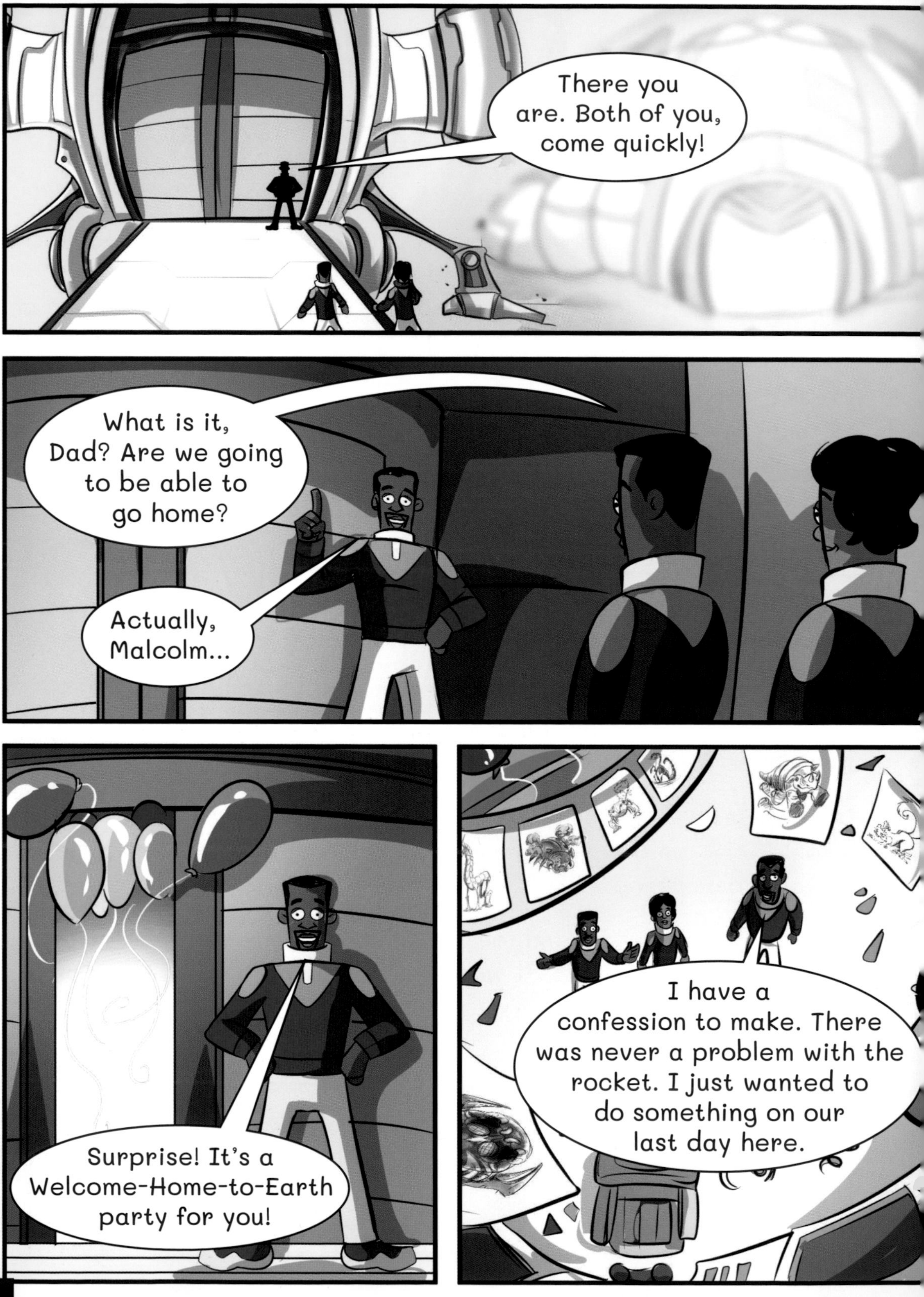
There you are. Both of you, come quickly!
What is it, Dad? Are we going to be able to go home?
Actually, Malcolm...
Surprise! It's a Welcome-Home-to-Earth party for you!
I have a confession to make. There was never a problem with the rocket. I just wanted to do something on our last day here.

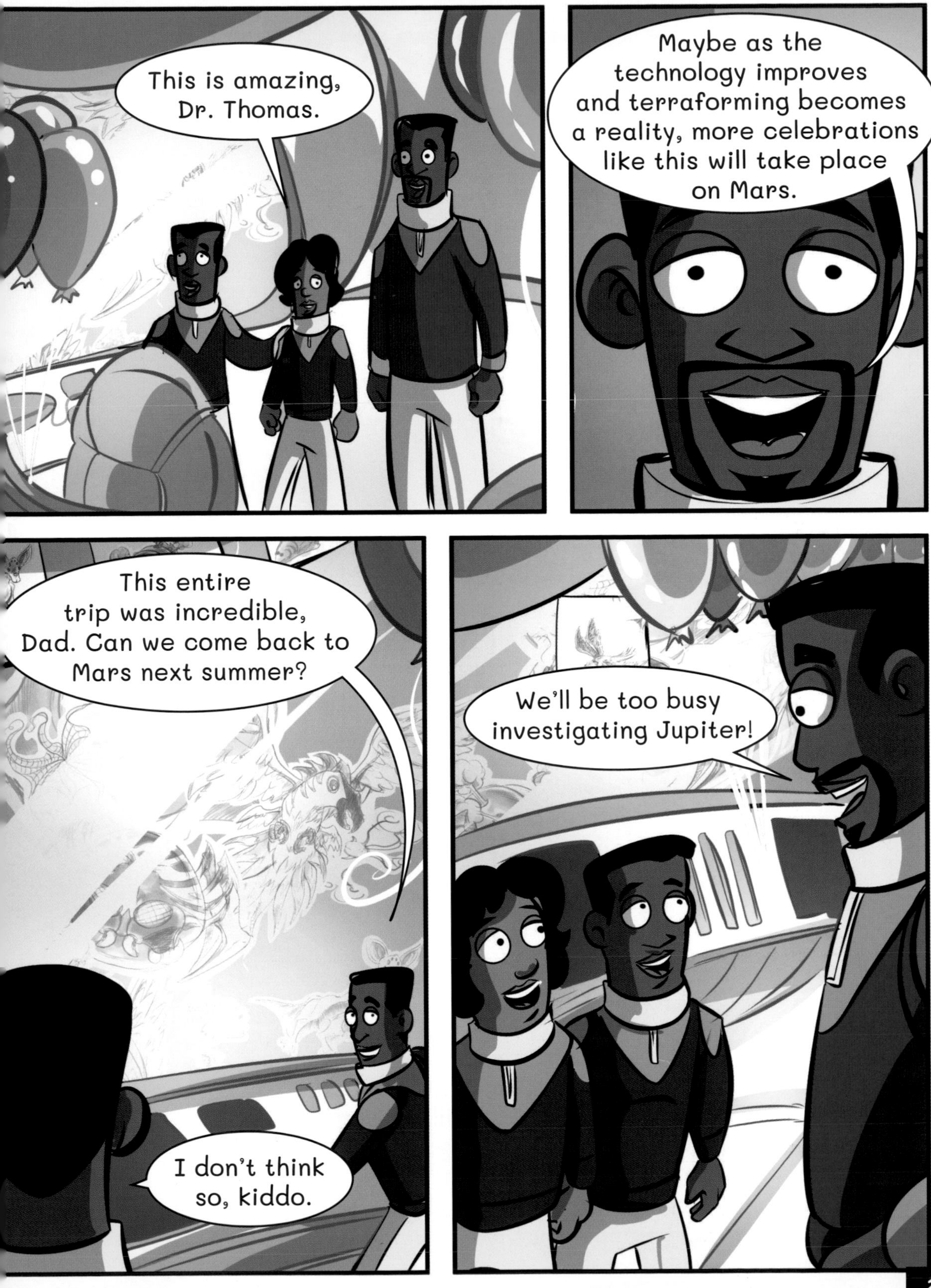
This is amazing, Dr. Thomas.
Maybe as the technology improves and terraforming becomes a reality, more celebrations like this will take place on Mars.
This entire trip was incredible, Dad. Can we come back to Mars next summer?
I don't think so, kiddo.
We'll be too busy investigating Jupiter!

MYSTERIOUS MARS MUD

There are countless mysteries to be discovered on Mars in the years to come. One mystery here on Earth is how potatoes can turn into m[...]

WHAT YOU NEED

- shredded potatoes
- mixing bowl
- hot water
- mixing spoon
- strainer
- large mixing bowl
- glass jar
- small bowl
- tonic water
- black ligh[...]

STEPS TO TAKE

1. Pour the shredded potatoes into the mixing bowl. Watch as an adu[...] pours hot water over the potatoes. Stir the potatoes.

2. Set the strainer onto the large mixing bowl. After the water cools, pour the potatoes into the strainer to separate the water from the potatoes. Set the strained water aside. Discard the potatoes.

3. After about 10 minutes, you will notice a thick white layer forming [...] the bottom of the bowl. Pour the water out. The white layer will rem[...]

4. Pour a bit of clean water into the white layer and mix it around. D[...] the mixture into the glass jar. Use the spoon to stir it around. Then s[...] aside for 10 minutes. That mysterious white layer will appear once ag[...]

5. Pour the water out. Set the glass jar aside for 2 days. The white lo[...] will turn into a powder.

6. Place a few spoonfuls of the powder into a bowl. Mix in the tonic water, starting with a small amount and adding more as needed. The [...] powder will become a goo that will harden when you handle it but tur[...] to liquid when you leave it alone.

7. Play with the goo under a black light. The tonic water has an ingredient calls quinine that makes it glow!

LEARN MORE

BOOKS

Bolte, Mari. *Exploring Mars*. Ann Arbor, MI: Cherry Lake Publishing, 2022.

MacCarald, Clara. *Colonizing Mars*. Lake Elmo, MN: Focus Readers, 2020.

WEBSITES

NASA: *Perseverance*
https://www.nasa.gov/perseverance

Learn about *Perseverance*'s mission to Mars and get all the latest news and discoveries.

Science Alert: What Is Mars?
https://www.sciencealert.com/mars

What is Mars? Find out about the geography of the Red Planet.

THE MARTIANS

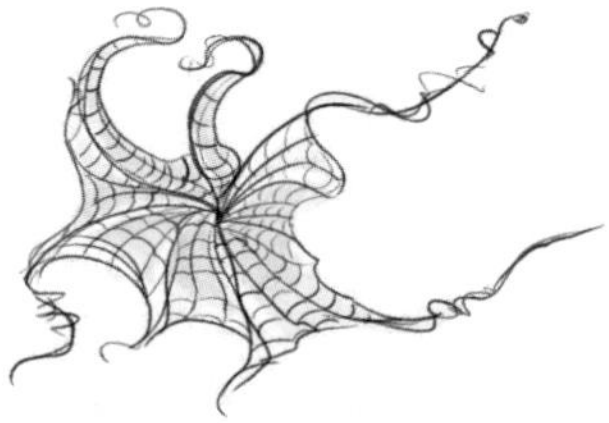

WEAVING WEEVILS

More fungus than insect, Malcolm imagines that this creepy-crawly Martian can camouflage itself as its own web and lure in prey.

LILAC BEETLES

With eerie sunken eyeballs and ability to spray a lilac scent, Malcolm views these Martian insects as residents of futuristic cities on Mars.

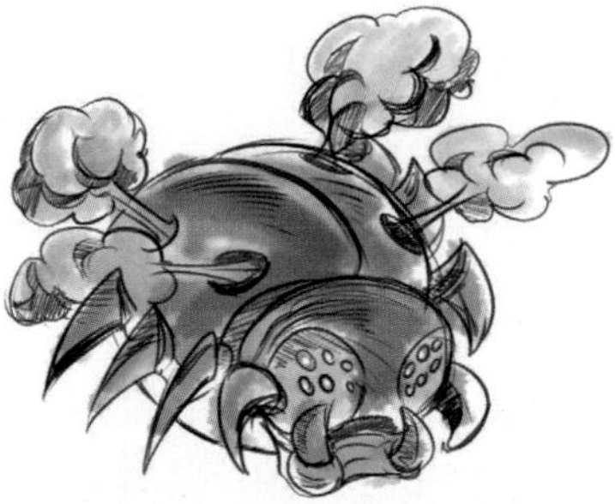

BIFOLD SPIDERS

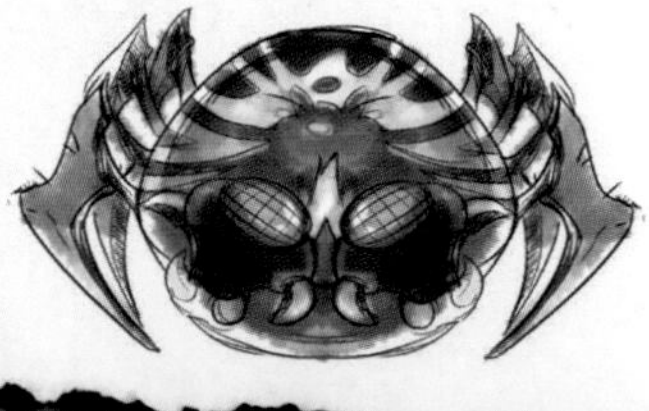

Proving that two heads are better than one, this Martian arachnid cooked up by Malcolm helps him to overcome his own fear of spiders.

GLOSSARY

abuela (uh-BWAY-luh) grandma in Spanish

camouflage (KAM-uh-flaj) to disguise or hide something

component (kom-PO-nuhnt) a part of a machine

cosmic radiation (KAZ-mik-ray-dee-AY shuhn) energy that travels through space at the speed of light

density (DEN-suh-tee) the measure of mass inside an object or substance

DNA (DEE ENN AY) molecule that contains the unique genetic code of living things

ecology (ee-KAH-luh-gee) the relationship between organisms and the environment

habitable (hab-IT-uh-buhl) a place that safe to live

microscopic (my-kroh-SKAH-pik) something so small it only be seen with a microscope

Morse code (MORS KOHD) a system of communication that uses dots and dash to represent letters and numbers

radiation (ray-dee-AY-shuhn) energy that travels through waves

rationing (RASH-uhn-ingh) to eat or dr a set amount

structural (STRUK-shuh-ruhl) relating to the structure of the ship

INDEX